Take Two,
A Smart-ass Mystery

by

John Ostapkovich

Take Two, A Smart-ass Mystery

ISBN: 978-1-62249-097-4

Published by
Biblio Publishing
BiblioPublishing.com

Contents

Disclaimer

This is a work of fiction. The characters are all the invention of my fevered imagination. Any resemblance to persons living or dead is pretty sad, actually.

While Philadelphia is a real place, the version presented here is as seen in a fun house mirror, made unreal for entertainment purposes, like Las Vegas.

Dedication

To my late friend Paul Rae. After the Challenger disaster, he tried to juggle the competing demands of being a good reporter and a good human being, which is a lot tougher than you might think.

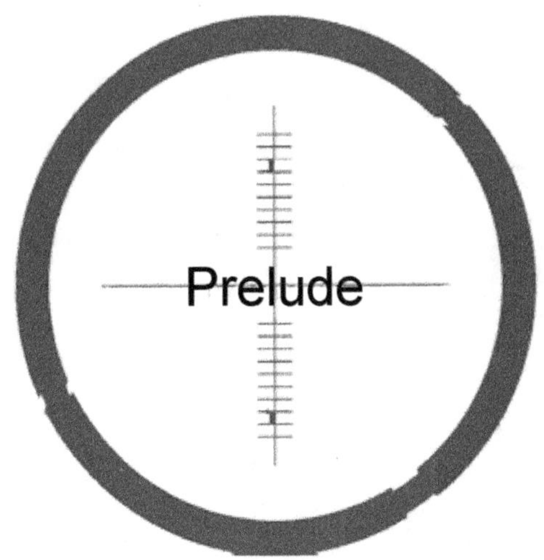

Prelude

The smell of iron swirled with bitter gun smoke, trapped in the echoing rapid transit tunnel. People scrambled, shouted and sobbed, but all I could hear was the pounding of my panicked heart. I dashed for cover, support pillar to pillar, my chest heaving with fear and effort. I glanced at my sleeve and found it sticky red for the second time that day, both stains probably due to the same lunatic who was chasing me, deep under the river.

I fled for my life, knowing that the third time blood got on my coat it would be mine.

Take Two, A Smart-ass Mystery

Chapter One: Monday

Waking up at 2:14 a.m. sucks. Waking up at 2:14 a.m. to an annoying phone sucks more. And being told to drag your aging, aching butt out of bed to cover some dumb-ass story, well, that's show biz.

The woman on the phone was polite enough. There's a big fire in Kensington, and she gave me the address. Big fire? Hell, that's urban renewal.

Jen didn't budge, God love/hate her. My wife could fall asleep in an elevator between floors, in an airplane before they were done with safety feature theater and anytime the announcer said, "Now pitching for the Phillies." I sat there for a moment looking at her, wondering how, if I was smart enough to get her to marry me, I was stupid enough to be working for a radio pirate. It's like being the last horseshoe salesman in town.

I was in a pickle. This fire had to be at least three alarms to trigger the phone call from our off-hours emergency radio monitoring service and, as the on-call reporter then, I was expected to go. But the station was all-network overnights. There was nobody minding the store until maybe 4 a.m. when Silcox found his way in from whatever bar or boudoir in which he'd spent half the night. I could just lie down for an hour, all right maybe a half hour, and be at the barbeque in plenty of time.

Nevertheless, I grabbed my glasses and rose from bed like a sleepwalker because that was pretty much true. The bathroom nightlight beckoned but when I had closed the door behind me and flipped the switch I was assaulted into wakefulness by bright globes and mirrors. All it needed was neon and it could have been Broadway.

A quick shower and shave completed, I was picking up steam. Yes, yes, this is a toothbrush and you put the tooth paste here. Shirt and pants were no problem and I accessorized with socks, shoes and a belt before heading out of the bedroom. A last glance at Jen and a peek into the kids' rooms, then it was downstairs to pat my jackets in the closet looking for keys. There were a bewildering number of places they hid and I swore it was a game to them.

My car didn't seem any happier to be awakened than I had been. It growled and grumbled but got with the program in a plume of exhaust and a dashboard sound and light show that reminded me of a pinball machine saying tilt.

I turned on the big news radio station. It was traitorous of me, listening to the enemy, but they were at least open all night, local all night, and while they also had no reporter at that hour their traffic service did a pretty good imitation of a scene-setter.

Be sure to avoid thus and such intersection due to fire department activity. Detours are posted. I, of course, was heading straight there.

There was nobody on I-95, which allowed me to further muster my thoughts. Street lamps began rushing by as I crossed the city line, adding a certain tempo to my deliberations. Get to the scene, work up to or hopefully through the police cordon, find the fire commander, get something official from him, some comments from the neighbors, a little siren or natural sound action if there is any and then set up shop in my mobile studio, also known as my dog-eared Honda.

If only I'd saved what I'd done during the last urban bonfire, or the one before that, I could have stayed home.

By the time I passed the Bridge Street exit, I could see what all the fuss would be about, a cantaloupe glow like all the city's streetlamps in one block. The radio traffic guy said it was now five alarms and fire crews were spending as much time squirting nearby structures as the burning one. I hoped no firefighters were inside. There was such a thing as too much news.

I parked a couple of blocks away, close enough to see the glare of the flames in row house windows but out of the general line of fire. If I'd had a station car (if we HAD station cars), I could have gone closer but what's the point? I was out of the Honda and, gear grabbed from the trunk, moving toward the fire in a moment. I stepped carefully over plump fire hoses bringing water in from blocks away, each little leak threatening to form a keester-kissing ice-patch for the unwary.

I noticed a couple of people on a front stoop, bundled up but enjoying the show. I pulled out my microphone and fired up the recorder.

"You guys see how this started?" I asked.

A woman with bloodshot eyes (or maybe it was just the fire) turned to me lazily, a cigarette dangling from one side of her dentally challenged mouth.

"Nah, but it's been burning like a motherfucker for an hour. Me and the Mister" indicating with a nod the other spectator "were watching Comedy Central, must have fallen asleep, then all of a sudden, woo, woo, woo, fire trucks and cops all over the place. I ain't seen a cop on this street in three weeks. How about you, Franny?" Franny grunted. "Takes something like this....." Her voice trailed off.

"What is or was that place?" I wondered.

"Shit." It was Franny this time. "That's been just about everything except City Hall. My grandpa worked there when it made locomotive parts for Baldwin. I think they had a still in there during the Depression. Clothing factory, PVC pipes, fuck, I think there's even a city recycling center in a corner of the place way around on McDougal. Mostly lately it's a warehouse although who'd want to store shit around here?"

"Okay, thanks guys." My microphone drooped post-coitally.

"Hey, we gonna be on the news?" asked the woman.

"Maybe," I responded, groping for my pen and notepad. I could edit their profanity but all that would be left would be prepositions. "What's your name?" They looked at one another as if they had just been cornered by store security.

"Irma."

"Frank."

"Last names?"

The man shrugged. "Logan."

"Thanks."

"Hey, when will this be on?"

"A little later this morning."

"What station?"

"WPN, 1620 AM."

"Fuck," said the woman. "Can't get AM in here for shit." She flicked her cigarette into the street where it sizzled and died in a puddle, extinguished along with her dream of celebrity.

I checked my watch. 3:18. Plenty of time. Too much time, really. I could be freezing before I even went on the air.

I walked a block toward the inferno, past bundled up neighbors chased from nearby homes, until January felt like March (much better) and then cut around the police line long enough to see a couple of firefighters not holding hoses or otherwise engaged. Probably officers.

I approached, mike down but visible. It saved a lot of explaining, so the front line cop let me through.

"Hi," I said to the fire officers, "who's in charge around here? Can you guys comment?"

They gave each other a look that I've learned from Jen means, it's your turn to change a diaper.

One faced me, lifting a clipboard to check some notes. "First call came in at 1:37. Engine 6, ladder 47 arrived 1:44, reported flames from lower floors....." This could go on all night.

"Excuse me, what's your name?" I could see his rank from his helmet and his last name stenciled on the jacket but I needed the first name as much as I needed to break him out of "fire-speak" which like its cousin "police-ese" is death-on-a-stick for radio.

"Lt. Henry Stempler, public information officer on the fire ground," he replied, but before he could get rolling again reading his logbook I tried to maneuver his comments into something that wouldn't bore the audience so much they'd wish they were on fire.

"What kind of building is that?"

"It's a four story, brick-fronted industrial structure, about a hundred years old, we understand. It's been subdivided, so there's mixed use, some e-commerce on the second floor, warehouse on the first."

"A city recycling center?"

"Yeah, that's around the other side where the fire is most intense."

There was a roar that caused us all to swing around. A plume of sparks leaped up from the far side of the fire. Tactical radios began blaring immediately and the other officer, a deputy chief by his insignia, stepped away to bark into his. His words also spilled out of the one in Lt. Stempler's hand.

"Captain Bevino, this is Chief Howard! What was that? Is everyone all right?" There was a pause in which the two men seemed to stretch toward the building, to lean in like someone cheating on an exam, just for a tiny peek at the answer.

The radios squawked together. "Wall collapse, sir, pretty much the entire west face. No injuries."

"Jesus," sighed Howard. Then he keyed the radio. "Good. Just keep everybody back. Let's all go home tonight."

It took a moment to recapture the spirit of the interview, to get back into the mundane give and take after a pants-wetting moment.

"Recycling," I prompted. "Old soda cans and the like?"

"Soda cans don't burn very well," said Lt. Stempler. "Old newspapers, cardboard and plastic burn like crazy."

"You think that's what's burning?"

He gave me a look. "Everything's burning. The building is a goner. Our main jobs at this point are to keep everybody safe and keep the fire from burning the neighborhood down." The money cut. I could see he regretted it as soon as he said it. Not that there was anything wrong with it, but it was just too direct, too painful and not fire-speak.

"That's it for now." He turned away and I stopped recording. Good for me, I exulted. Good nat sound and the money cut, bam bam. Another reason I'd rather be lucky than good. And the art of the stupid question didn't hurt either.

If you ask stupid questions, you often get better answers because people explain things to you like you're an idiot. They connect A to B to C in a way they wouldn't if they thought you could see the connection yourself. That way you get them to make the connection for an audience that may or may not be paying attention. And may or may not be composed of idiots.

I checked my watch. 4:07. Time to make the donuts. I patted myself down for my cell phone and called the producer, Silcox.

Eaton Shaw Silcox was a Princeton frat boy turned into a Philly fat boy, a guy who never met a cheese steak he didn't like and, washed down with a brewski or twoski, even better. He was loud, proud and completely convinced that he knew shit when he couldn't have found it with his head up his ass. The one thing he had going for him career-wise was a complete lack of remorse for being a suck-up. He even had designer kneepads.

"Newsroom, Silcox," he answered. "That you, Beanie?" The name is Bernie, you asshole!

"Yes, it's me."

"You at the fire?" No, I'm in my jammies, at home in bed, like anyone with half a brain would be!

"You bet. This thing's toast. We just had a wall collapse. Scared the crap out of everybody. All they're doing is controlling the burn."

"Yeah, right...." His voice trailed off, distracted, as if I was interrupting something far more important. "Call me at 4:30. I'll put you on live." Be still, my heart.

"See you." I cut the connection. This was just what I'd expected, the regular drill. I'd nursemaid this thing for another few hours then file a report and some voice cuts and that would be that.

Since I had a little time to kill, I zigzagged down some narrow streets to eyeball the other side of the building. Although some of it looked like an evil jack-o-lantern with glowing window eyes, I was stopped in my tracks by the sight of the portion that had collapsed. It truly glared like the gateway to hell with souls writhing in the open fire. Flames roared in the center of the structure, barely contained by walls roasted into instability. Bricks, furniture, support beams, walls, floors, toilets, tables, computers, recyclables and anything else joined the grand old slag dismissing firefighters' fountains like the merest mist. A dog pissing on a tree down the block was doing as much good. I could feel the skin on my face drying in the flickering heat.

At 4:29 I called Silcox back and he hit a button plugging my cell phone into the studio control board where Anthony Freeman and Tina Lowell co-anchored our little slice of heaven. At this time of day, the local news consisted of ten-minute blocks inserted at the hour and half-hour into the all-news feed from the Cheapo Broadcasting Network. That wasn't its actual name, of course, but it was the kind of thing you end up with when you worked for a crook.

"In the news at this hour," I heard Tina say on cue-back through the phone, "a six alarm industrial blaze in

Kensington chases residents into the January chill. We'll have a live report. The Mayor declares a moratorium on the Governor's moratorium on riverfront development and the Flyers lose ground in a divisional clash with New Jersey."

Anthony picked up with the weather forecast, which, imagine this, was cold with a chance of snow, cold with a chance of ice and cold with a chance of cold. Why did we bother?

Tina was back on an instant later. "That six alarmer is still burning in Kensington." I took a breath, and looked up again into the inferno, trying to spot inspiration. "Let's get the latest live from We're Philly's News reporter Bernie Gaston. Bernie..."

Show time....

Chapter Two

Five live shots and two and a half hours later, the fire had died down and lost all its color to the gray January dawn. I had retreated to my car to ward off frostbite. The fire ground was a winter wonderland with ice bearding lights, signs, railings, and the occasional fireman squatted down taking a break. The building was no longer ablaze but what was left between its teetering outer walls steamed under the continued deluge, the fire's orange anger doused into monochrome surrender.

I had gotten some more sound with neighbors (they were shocked, absolutely shocked), another sound bite or two with the Lieutenant and retreated to my car in hopes of producing a couple of spots. Once I defrosted my fingers, my laptop ran off the cigarette lighter as I alternated between a word processor to write the script, my recorder to voice the track and the Sound Forge application to mix the elements into a finished piece. I wondered if I could slip out early and get a nap once the adrenaline rush faded.

I had just hit the "send" button to e-mail the second story back to the newsroom when there was a rap at the window that nearly caused me to drop my computer on the floor. I swung around to see a policeman pointing his nightstick at me.

"Hey, Jimmy Olsen, get a move on before I write you up." I still hadn't gotten much of a look at the face since the windows were pretty fogged up but the voice....

"Hi, Frank," I said dully. "Imagine meeting you here."

Frank Tierney was my brother-in-law, the husband of Jan who was the twin sister of Jen who I had left soundly, sanely sleeping at home. Frank was an all right guy for a cop, a little gruff, a little my-way-or-the-highway and a lot into the thin blue line. Police and reporters are not the best of friends. I try to be understanding about how they have an important job to do but so do we. Half the time, they react as if each case belongs to them, like it's their lunch or something, and to part with even a morsel is painful.

I put the laptop on the seat next to me and cranked down the window.

"How long have you been out here?"

"All fucking night," Frank replied, clipping his nightstick back on his belt. "You know, people are surprisingly ungrateful when you pound on their door at 2 in the morning and tell them to get out or they might die."

"It's bound to be a shock."

"Shock? Fuck, living near that firetrap? We had L&I out here six times in the last few months for this violation or that. It was practically arson-by-invitation."

"You saying this was arson?" He tensed up. Whoa, I thought, turn off Mr. Reporter for a moment. You know how he gets.

"Hey, this is all off-the-record. Let's just say, I wouldn't be surprised if the fire marshal figures out this started in three or four places at once. But what do I know?"

What, indeed, I asked myself. Officer Frank Tierney had been a street cop for 12 years and his chance of advancement was pretty much zero. If he were going to move up, he'd have done so already. He was not exactly a highly placed source on any of this, although I had to agree about the possibility of arson. The Lieutenant had said as much and even that wasn't a news flash.

"Don't worry, I'm not quoting you," I assured him. "What time you get off?"

He shrugged. "It was supposed to be half an hour ago, but they don't want to bring the day shift over here for an hour or two. I can use the overtime anyway. This isn't a big month for flowers."

Jan and Jen ran a florist shop together. Christmas was big but that was a fading memory. The bouquets had died, the toys were busted and even the boxes they came in had been recycled. About the only thing that brightened the business from now to Valentine's Day was cop break-ups and cop funerals.

JJ's Blue Ribbon was located in the City's Far Northeast, an area where lots of cops and firefighters lived. It was as close to the suburbs they could get and still keep their jobs, due to that pesky rule that they had to reside in Philadelphia. Some of them, with homes backing up to Poquessing Creek, could see the Promised Land but, like Moses, never live there.

Jan and Jen were cop-connected, the go-to girls for sentiment and ceremony. The holiday season had been pretty good but January could be long and lean.

Cop marriages were notoriously rocky. The stress of the job, the odd, unpredictable hours, the low pay and the camaraderie that many a spouse could not appreciate made the cycle of break-up and make-up a steady source of business. This bud's for you.

Of course, working for a dirt-bag radio station was no prize either. At least cops had the prospect of a quick death at the hands of a criminal, after which their memory would be enshrined in the local Valhalla. For me, death would come not with a bang, but a yawn.

"Good to see you, Frank," I said, trying to wrap this up. It wasn't that I wanted to go back to the station but it was as good an excuse as any to bolt.

"Yeah, you too, Bernie. Hey, you coming over on Saturday?" His dad's birthday party.

"You bet." I faked enthusiasm. "What can we get him?"

Frank grinned conspiratorially. "How about a sex toy? He's in that retirement home and it's wall to wall gray pussy."

"Viagra it is. Or something with batteries?"

"You got the idea." Frank flicked his index finger at me like he was firing off a round. He popped the top of the car with the palm of his hand and began to walk off. "See you, Jimmy Olsen."

I sighed as he left. That was stressful. It wasn't just that I didn't quite know how to interact with him but I got the feeling from Jen that she didn't either and, by extension, that something wasn't quite right with Jan. We didn't talk about it. Maybe even Jan and Jen didn't but that would create quite a strain, pitting the incredible bond twins have against the keep-things-in-the-"family" ethic of the police.

But something was up. "Jimmy Olsen" would have bet his cub reporter credentials on it.

I flipped open my cell phone and dialed news central. Silcox answered and I told him about the reports he'd find in the email account. Did he want anything else?

"I don't but TBC wants to see you."

Fuck me with a fork. TBC was code for "The Big Cheese" or Warren Peter Nash, the owner of the station who was, well, let's be honest, a criminal. Actually, a supremely egotistical criminal. On billboards, it looks as if our call letters, WPN, mean "We're Philly's News", a ridiculous claim on its face since we were about as popular as a dog fart, but they actually were his initials. Self-absorption and amorality was a bad combination.

"What about?"

"Dunno. He said to tell you. I told you. He said he'd be in about nine."

"Me too," I responded like a man being shown the really, really fine work on his gallows. You had to admire the craftsmanship. Ending the call, I started the car and retreated from the neighborhood the way I'd come in.

WPN's studios were neither centrally located nor posh but, thank God for small favors, not in Philadelphia.

Nothing against the city, mind you. I'd been here most of my life other than that brief, pay-your-dues experience in Colorado, but if you lived or worked in the city you paid the wage tax. If you lived and worked outside, you did not. It's money in my pocket, no more, no less. Of course, Nash didn't do it for me. He did it so he didn't have to pay city business taxes.

Some broadcasting operations had nice, new buildings that were landmarks. Two TV stations even sat right across the street from one another on City Avenue, one in Philadelphia, the other in Bala by virtue of the city line that ran down the middle of the street.

Others were located in gleaming Center City office towers or landscaped suburban professional plazas, wedged in between a proctologist and an orthodontist.

We, on the other hand, were stuck on a scrubby patch of no man's land in Whitemarsh, in the Schuylkill River flood plain, across the railroad tracks, behind Nash's truck warehouse, in a decrepit building once featured in Hovels Today magazine. "We're Philly's News", my ass. We're Philly's bastard son and dotty old uncle rolled up into one.

I pulled into the pothole-pitted parking lot, dodging an 18-wheeler evidently driven by someone with Tourette's syndrome judging from the language I could hear even through closed windows. That I found a parking place was not as remarkable as that it was actually on pavement which was actually plowed of the depressingly brown dregs of snow that lined it.

The "main building" was a squat one-story brick structure with all the personality of chewed gum. That was where Nash kept his office and his underlings including a mincing nephew who answered phones with a kind of androgynous severity, like Bette Davis after a lungful of smoke.

I bypassed the newsroom for now, eager to get this meeting over with. Years ago, I got fired from my first job out of college a few hours into my shift. I'd arrived at my regular time of 11 a.m. for afternoon news duty and the receptionist greeted me with, "Bernie, I'm so sorry."

I said, "For what?"

She said, "Oops." But that meant when I was summoned to meet that version of TBC I wasn't surprised when I was not given a raise, but shown the door.

I've avoided receptionists ever since but Jen says I'm just being paranoid.

So I went in the back entrance, past the equipment room and his and hers crappers. The water fountain looked like something left over from Roman times, in Pompeii.

TBC's office was across the threadbare lobby and I had some hope of avoiding Nephew Lorne who was on the potty-break-per-minute plan, but there he was, leafing through a travel magazine while telling someone on the phone how just mind-numbingly busy he was.

"Oh, Bernie," he said just as I thought I was home free. "My uncle wants to see you." He never missed a chance to let you know he was connected.

"Yes, I know," I said evenly. "Is now good?"

"I'll see." He whispered something into the phone, put that caller on hold and hit a button on the small console in front of him. "Uncle Warren, Bernie's here." Lorne nodded and turned back to me. "Go on in."

I tried to calm myself, to not visualize the words "Abandon hope all ye who enter" over the door to his office, and my feet took me right to the threshold. I stuck my head in.

"Mr. Nash, you wanted to see me?"

The man who looked up from his dark walnut desk was pushing 60 and it had definitely pushed back. It's not just that he was overweight, bald, bifocaled and sweaty. It's not just that he had a malevolent glare and stubby fingers good for manipulating nothing but people's lives. And it's not just that working in radio is like constantly perching at the end of the pirate's plank, waiting for the poke of a sword. It's all that and the fact that when I said Nash was a crook, I meant he'd ripped off suppliers, taken a cut of items that fell off the backs of trucks, screwed the working man and the banker and anybody who would give him something for 10% down. He'd been taken to court six times in the five years I worked for him and both the Feds and some investors were baying just outside the doors now.

Naturally, not one word of that had ever appears on We're Philly's News.

"Sit," he said, motioning me to a chair. "Bernie, that was nice work at the fire this morning, nice imagery."

"Thanks," I said, not that I meant it or thought he did. "What can I do for you?" If getting your head chopped off is the feature presentation, there's no need to sit through the previews of coming attractions.

"Funny you should put it that way." He leaned back and clasped his hands behind his head. Ooh, the "we're all friends here" power position. "You know, I'm sure, that my business activities are under investigation." I nodded. Uh-oh. "They are going to be deposing people around here over the next few weeks. I tried to keep them out of the newsroom, claiming First Amendment or something but they want what they want." He put his hands back on the desk and shrugged. "I could have just issued a memo (actually, I'm about to send an email) but I wanted to tell you personally." He paused. "Because you're first."

Get out that fork again. "What on earth do they think I know?"

"I told them you don't know nothin'," he lapsed into a really bad gangster voice, "but they were insistent. More to the point, HE was insistent." He paused and I gestured, who? "An FBI agent named Gary Semenov, Semyenoff..."

"Gary Semyenovic," I ventured. It was like looking at the truck about to run you down and realizing, hey, I know the driver. I hung my head a moment.

If no good deed goes unpunished, neither does good reporting. Semyenovic had been the lead agent on a big drug bust aboard a private plane at the airport a few years back. They'd done the whole dog and pony show in a hangar to announce it, with a table full of plastic-wrapped blocks of cocaine, and color 8x10's of the somewhat smirky suspects. That was at 10 a.m. and we in the media all stampeded off to report it. By 1 p.m., the story took a whiplash turn, when defense lawyers waving legal briefs summoned us to just outside the Federal Courthouse where they had gotten the whole damn thing thrown out on a technicality, that being a bad search warrant obtained by (come on now, who else?) Gary Semyenovic.

That everything I and all the other reporters wrote and said was true is of little consequence since it was now his face on TV, evading questions but not the inevitable bureaucratic responsibility. Special Agent Semyenovic was not fired but certainly became a little less special. He'd been reassigned to financial crimes where he would face down anti-social accountants on a daily basis. It was the stuff of legends.

And now he was going to get a crack at me, under oath. Oh, boy. If there was one thing that the whole Whitewater investigation had proven, it was that once they get you under oath they can ask you any damn thing they want about any damn thing they want and you'd better not lie because even if you did nothing else wrong perjury is a felony.

"When?" I asked.

"Tomorrow," Nash said as he shoved a subpoena across at me. I glanced at it. I was "commanded" to appear.

"Should I get a lawyer?"

"I can't advise you on that one, Bucko. I always have an attorney in the room representing my interests but you may be okay without one."

"Forget that. I expect you'll hire one for me, since I'm only in this because of you. Our interests would seem to coincide."

He glared, perhaps taken aback, or perhaps doing a quick cost-benefit analysis. "Sure, that's only fair. Tell Lorne who you want and he'll make the arrangements."

"Okay, then." I rose and turned to go.

"Hey, Bernie," he said behind me, "it's good to have friends."

Chapter Three

I emerged from TBC's office looking for someone to hate and there was Lorne, still on the phone, pretending to work.

"Excuse me," I said and he looked at me as if I was a fascinating new species of shellfish. He whispered something into the phone and put it on hold.

"Yes?"

"Mr. Nash says you're supposed to arrange for a lawyer for me during a deposition I have at 9 tomorrow morning, FBI, 600 Chestnut St., 8th floor. Mr. Nash says I get to pick so see if you can get Jack Speer. If not him, then Hollis Townsend. They're both in the book but if you run into trouble I have their numbers."

Lorne made a show of writing this down.

"Will that be all?" He sounded as if I was as rude as a car crashing through the kitchen window.

The newsroom was only a few steps away but it felt like miles carrying a piano on my back. This was just great. The deposition could be a ball-buster, especially since I really didn't know anything about Nash's activities, legal or otherwise.

Broadcasting was a strange industry where the people who create what appears to be the product generally have no idea of the business end of things. Remember, our "product" at WPN was, as far as the audience was concerned, news, a repeating hour-long programming wheel including weather, traffic and sports. Most of what we put out was national. Hit a key on the control board and the network was at the helm. But for five minutes every half-hour most of the day, and ten minutes during morning and evening rush hours, our little newsroom drove the show.

But that product was, of course, free. We gave our work away, the theory being that it was so fascinating and valuable that listeners would stick around during this brief word from our sponsor. That's what the sales department sold, a moment of the audience's time, so the money was handled by people who never produced even a peep of programming, and the air staff never saw a dime of the money other than what was in our checks.

The newsroom was tucked away in a corner of the building with a great view of the trucks out back when the blinds weren't down. It was roughly rectangular with desks along the walls, computers on the desks and tangles of wires underneath that would appall any fire inspector. There was a single door into the studio, which contained the control board with microphone and two other mikes with on-off switches only. It was like Radio Shack in a box.

Silcox looked up from his computer, phone pressed to his ear. He held up one index finger to indicate, give me a moment.

I plunked down in what loosely might be called my chair. It was only force of habit since we had people cycling in and out of here 24/7. No one could say whose bottom was the last to warm this seat.

I logged on to the newsroom computer system, which, when it worked, was a marvel. It married our written copy and our audio so that anchoring was now the simplest part of the job. Good thing, since our anchors were simple.

There were a couple of in-office emails, including the one Nash said he was just about to send. That was going to be a real morale booster. Depositions all around! There were two emails from state agencies about things that may or may not be interesting or local or even true. You always had to check. There was one from Jen, probably fired off once she awoke and saw me gone.

I clicked it open. It was a reminder that she had a volunteer gig at the library that evening, there's meat loaf in the fridge, the kids will be at her mom's and need to be picked up by six.

I looked at the clock. It was barely 9:30 and I could tell it was going to be a long day.

"Bernie." It was Silcox, having put down the phone. "That was the Mayor's office. He's going to have a thing at 11:30 about the fire. Room 202. Be there or be square."

Silcox said that tag line every single time. If it had ever been clever, which I doubted, it had long since reached its expiration date.

"Okay," I acknowledged, not wanting to prolong the misery, but he didn't take the hint.

"Look, I don't want to be a dick." Too late. "But Gina called out and I need you to make a couple of calls on this." He handed me a fax.

"This" was a thumb sucker press release for a Martin Luther King Day service project, dozens, hundreds, thousands of earnest young people putting down their drugs and guns for a day of pretending to fix up the school they were so busy avoiding the rest of the time.

Oh, well. It should be easy enough.

I picked up the phone and dialed the contact number. One ringy-dingy, two, three, four, and voicemail picks up. "Hi," the recording said, "this is Marc Solarz of Freedom's Light. I'll be on vacation from the 10th to the 15th but I'll be checking in for messages....." Blah, blah, blah.

I hated it when P.R. loads put out a press release inviting media attention and then made themselves scarce when you tried to do something about it. I hung up and dialed the main number for Freedom's Light. No one answered, of course, unless you count one of those automated systems that could misdirect your call better than any mere human. The group's executive director was referenced repeatedly, almost fawningly, in the press release and a moment after I punched his extension, a voice answered.

"Mr. Hanson's office. Brenda speaking."

"Hi, this is Bernie Gaston over at WPN. I'm looking to get a couple of minutes with Mr. Hanson about next Monday's MLK clean-up events."

"Oh, well, you should be talking to Marc Solarz. He's our media contact."

"He's on vacation, at least that's what his voicemail says."

"But he will be checking in. His voicemail also says that." Great, consider me put in my place. "I hope you don't mind but Mr. Hanson wants the press handled by Marc. Please leave him a message and he will get back to you."

"Bu..." was about all I managed to get out before I was once again listening to Marc Solarz' explanation of how he was out but really in. Catch-22, anyone?

I left my name and number, despite a sinking feeling that this was going to be a telephone tag circle jerk. I'd go out on my next story. He'd call. I'd get back from the story. I'd call and he'd be out again. Repeat until totally frustrated.

"This may or may not happen today," I told Silcox who looked as if it were my fault that the Freedom's Light people were dim bulbs. "What else you got?" He shuffled some stuff on the desk and then handed me his gold mine of research, the morning paper.

"The Inky says they're expecting a major ski weekend coming up." No shit, really? A three-day weekend in January and people go skiing? Alert the media! I demand a recount!

"Sure," I responded and took the section of the paper he offered. I scanned the article. They'd had a reporter up in the Poconos go to at least one ski mountain and maybe two or three, judging from the quotes from skiers. I was supposed to duplicate the story, quick and dirty, by phone. Oh, well....

Following the paper was a time-honored tradition in radio news. They have a hundred reporters, maybe more. We have, on a good day, three or four. Newspaper people consider themselves the keepers of the journalistic torch and they do break their share of stories, but the big fire that morning got about one column-inch on the front page because of deadline karma. For the best fire story, TV was the place to look. TV loves flames.

But radio had the benefit of quick turn-around. Point me to some copy in the computer or give me the flimsiest ad lib and we could get it on the air while newspapers were yelling "Stop the presses!" or "Great Caesar's ghost!" or whatever they said when re-arranging the front page, and TV producers were fighting like cats in a bag trying to find someone willing to make a decision.

Quick and dirty, now that's radio news!

I typed "Pocono ski areas" in the Internet search field and got half a dozen hits in a blink. Not being a skier, I didn't know one from another but I picked one close to the Northeast extension and dialed the main number. Here, because this was a place that actually wanted phone calls, an actual person answered and connected me to the general manager.

His assistant was much friendlier than the one at Freedom's Light and after a couple minutes on hold I was connected to Charles Van Dros who was just gushing with enthusiasm at the chance for a free commercial in Philadelphia. Don't kid yourself, that's what this was.

I asked his permission to record the conversation, as per Pennsylvania law and common courtesy, and opened an audio file in the computer to accommodate it. We chatted for five or six minutes of entirely forgettable blather before I signed off.

Now, the magic of radio, taking five pounds of poop, or ten or twenty and putting it in a snack Baggie (tm) called a 45 second report. I'll spare you the details of this story but here's an example. You've heard of Lincoln's Gettysburg Address, one of the most poignant, and shortest, Presidential speeches ever.

Take Two, A Smart-ass Mystery

Here's the text:

Four score and seven years ago our fathers brought forth on this continent, a new nation, conceived in Liberty, and dedicated to the proposition that all men are created equal.
Now we are engaged in a great civil war, testing whether that nation, or any nation so conceived and so dedicated, can long endure. We are met on a great battle-field of that war. We have come to dedicate a portion of that field, as a final resting place for those who here gave their lives that that nation might live. It is altogether fitting and proper that we should do this.
But, in a larger sense, we can not dedicate -- we can not consecrate -- we can not hallow -- this ground. The brave men, living and dead, who struggled here, have consecrated it, far above our poor power to add or detract. The world will little note, nor long remember what we say here, but it can never forget what they did here. It is for us the living, rather, to be dedicated here to the unfinished work, which they who fought here have thus far so nobly advanced. It is rather for us to be here dedicated to the great task remaining before us -- that from these honored dead we take increased devotion to that cause for which they gave the last full measure of devotion -- that we here highly resolve that these dead shall not have died in vain -- that this nation, under God, shall have a new birth of freedom -- and that government of the people, by the people, for the people, shall not perish from the earth.

Legend says it took him less than 5 minutes to read and it left the audience wondering, what? Did he write that on an envelope on the way up here? I got all gussied up and came down here for this?

So let's do a little experiment. We'll turn this into a radio news story. To start, where's the money cut? The first and last lines are good, poetic, pithy but long. Every second we give over to Abe is one less for me to provide the context for this. So how about we go with "that from these honored dead we take increased devotion to that cause for which they gave the last full measure of devotion"?

Problem. How long did he take to say that? There are no recordings, so let's guess 11 seconds, read in a sonorous politician's pace with pauses. Now, with most people, I could just cut out the pauses, snip, snip, snip on the computer and now it's 8 seconds and livelier, but old tradition says you're not allowed to edit the President, so we're stuck.

We begin at the beginning, the anchor introduction, intro or lede:

President Lincoln today hailed the sacrifices of those who died in the battle of Gettysburg four months ago. We're Philly's News reporter Bernie Gaston was there....

Now imagine my recorded voice and the soundbite of Abe:

In a brief speech before seemingly all of Gettysburg's 2400 residents whose town and nearby land still bear the scars of the battle, the President dedicated the Soldiers National Cemetery at a place where more than seven thousand troops died over three days of combat in July. Mr. Lincoln said that the sacrifices made by soldiers here speak for themselves as history unfolds...

"that from these honored dead we take increased devotion to that cause for which they gave the last full measure of devotion."

The President closed with a stirring line about dedication to preserving a nation with government, quoting, "of the people, by the people, for the people." Some in the crowd expressed reservations about the speech inasmuch as the

Take Two, A Smart-ass Mystery

President did not distinguish between Union and Confederate casualties.
Bernie Gaston, WPN, Gettysburg.

That's it, a boiled down version of a really short speech. It gets progressively tougher. If the guy goes on for half an hour or 45 minutes and tackles multiple topics, you still get 45 seconds. A daylong court hearing for the latest mad raper-stomper, 45 seconds. Whatever it is, 45 seconds. Or less. Don't forget, or less.
But writing the skiing story wasn't nearly that hard. It was a puff piece. Holiday weekend, skiers flock, our resort has the goods, blah, blah, blah. But it filled some airtime and kept me busy until it was time to go to City Hall.
Adventure awaited.

Chapter Four

As I drove from the station to City Hall, I tried to forget the minefield I was about to enter. Give the Feds too little and they'd think I was lying or they'd start digging around for what I might have done, like smoked weed back in the day or mixed up a little home-brew amphetamines for a college cramfest. I mean, unless you'd done something wrong sometime, you'd probably never done anything, period. Give the Feds too much (which would be extremely made up) and I'd be looking for work, blackballed in a very small business.

My route unavoidably took me on the Schuylkill Expressway. That's pronounced school-kill, if you want to get technical, or skookl, if you want Philadelphia-ese. It was A) an amazing engineering achievement and B) a real piece of crap, all at the same time. For much of its length, it was four lanes of winding highway jammed between a steep hill on one side and a watch-that-first-step drop on the other down to the river from which it gets its name.

Some exits were on the right, some on the left. I swore the highway's signs said things like: Montgomery Drive, 1 mile, Girard Avenue, 2 miles, Roosevelt Expressway, you just missed it, putz! You really had to know.

Philadelphia City Hall sits squarely astride two major streets, detouring them both in a metaphor of municipal government. It is an enormous edifice that used to house executive and legislative offices as well as courts, but they moved criminal trials to a new building across the street so much of it was then devoted to the Museum of Graft. Not really, but it should have been.

It is the tallest freestanding masonry structure in the world, no girders, took 30 years to build and once was cleaned of 37 tons of pigeon shit. Put your fist on the table, and raise your middle finger. That's about what it looks like except it has a square courtyard where vagrants and crazy people hold daily urination Olympics. Atop the upraised middle finger stands a statue of William Penn, the founder of Pennsylvania and designer of colonial Philadelphia, the exact center of which, Center Square, was City Hall's location. From his perch, he stares roughly northeast, toward New York, and is probably thinking, why the hell didn't I land there?

I parked in a press zone on the Ben Franklin Parkway, Philadelphia's self-declared Champs-Elysees. It was a pretty street with a fountain plaza on one end with City Hall looming caddy-corner and the imposing Philadelphia Museum of Art (yes, with the Rocky steps) on the other. But Paris' most famous boulevard teems with life, sidewalk cafes, shopping and joie de vivre. Our Parkway was mostly something you drove along. It was a tiring walk past its many museums with almost no place to wet your whistle or take a break, much less a leak.

I didn't have to walk that far, just across Love Park, which is famous not only for the sculpture which says

LO
VE

but for the critters that the city has tried so hard to remove. Not rats, skateboarders who loved the park's multiple levels, railings and stone benches so much that it became an international magnet for sidewalk surfers. But pedestrians and brown baggers were pissed at teens shouting "Kowabunga!" and things not even remotely complimentary as they careened past, so the City banned the skateboarders and promised them a new skate park. I think they're still waiting.

I stood in line with the hoi polloi at the security entrance, got my sticker and climbed the curving staircase in the Northeast corner rather than wait on the rickety elevators to go up just one floor

Room 202 was where the Mayor held forth. It was called the Reception Room and with its gilded ceiling, chandeliers and wall-mounted portraits of every mayor Philadelphia has ever had it is both fascinating and intimidating. Probably by design.

I was neither the first nor last reporter to arrive. I plunked down my gear bag near the mult-box and plugged in for a sound check. A mult-box is a multiple connector, so there can be just one microphone at the podium and one wire running away from it. It's a much cleaner look than what you see overseas where you'll have the President of East Jeppip, unshaven and sleep-deprived, facing a table with about nine thousand mike flags on it. Jeez Louise, you guys make the electronics. Buy some for a change.

Sound check complete (there was a hum, but there always was) I looked to see who else was there. A couple of the TV stations had only sent photographers who would record the news conference for someone to go over later. But two TV's actually had reporters, Sarah Tilson and Garrison Watts. Both were pretty good, turning in their share of "scoops", but mostly just churning out solid reporting show after show, day after day. Who, what, where, when, why, what does it mean and why should I care?

Sarah was tall and shapely with a TV-pretty face and a penchant for short skirts and fuck-me pumps. Hollywood portrays people that turned-out as vapid, and she could play that game but don't let it fool you. She knew the art of the dumb question and used her looks to get past people's defenses so she could ask it. Fans would come up to her and say, you look better on TV, or you look better in person, but that's the whole thing about TV-pretty. It was like plastic mixed with brass, where a little Maybelline and blue tinted lenses can turn eye contact into foreplay. That was good news reading, all blown up on 50-inch screens, but in person it also encompassed some body English. I'd seen her work a police captain into a corner just by swiveling her hips this way or that and he was happy to talk.

Garrison was another story, a 50-ish African American who had been a cop until he'd been hurt in a crash responding to a call. He retired on disability but soon started reporting for one of the papers and with his contacts in the police department developed some major breaking stories. He was easy on the eyes in a trusted-uncle sort of way, so he anchored weekend nights and reported three days a week, mostly events like this where there was some cops-and-robbers connection. Just having him in the room kept the brass honest.

There were a couple of radio reporters, one from a college station who looked in fear for her life, two newspaper scribes, each adopting an "It's tough to be superior" attitude as they pretended to read what little was interesting in their respective rags.

I said "hi" to Watts' cameraman, a skinny black guy with a nervous energy that made him seem like he was Jack in the Box and someone was turning the crank. He had a couple of kids too and we often traded stories about how these creatures from inner space had made it so we came to work to get a rest.

Watts sauntered over, sort of half full-of-himself after a handshake or two with a couple of the police and fire bigs. He knew everyone and, on the police side at least, probably ever since they were in uniform scooping up winos on Code Blue winter nights. Now, they'd just order it done by someone else.

Watts was beginning to tell an anecdote one had related when there was a rustle in the doorway and the room fell into an expectant hush as Hizzoner breezed in. Mayor Charles Gilroy was not an Everyman, but he played one on TV and in public settings like this. He glad-handed like someone moving down the reception line with one eye on the cake. With a JD from Penn, he could be making a lot more money than what being Mayor paid, but he loved the spotlight, the brighter, the better, more than even a partnership at Dewey, Cheatem and Howe.

A tallish man in his early 40's, Gilroy was a light-skinned African-American, in this case a literal expression because his dad was heir to some Main Line money and about as white as you could get, while his mom, from Liberia, eschewed dresses and business suits for some get-up that made her look like a vertical fruit salad.

Gilroy got to the podium among scattered applause from those who knew whom to thank for their phony baloney jobs. He slapped a folder down with such force that anyone listening to the audio feed on headphones winced. He grinned. My bad. I started my recorder.

Normally, Gilroy began every appearance with the same three tired jokes, but skipped straight to the meat of the matter this time.

"Ladies and gentlemen, this is a Moment of Special Gravity here in the City of Philadelphia." You could just tell he was capitalizing things. "This morning's warehouse fire in Kensington was, as many of you no doubt suspect, arson. I'll have more to say on this in a moment, but first let's get Fire Commissioner Bailey up here with the nitty gritty."

Alvin Bailey was huge, playing the part of mastiff to the Mayor's Jack Russell terrier. He was second-generation PFD. When Bailey was a teenager, his father had died in a smoky skyscraper fire after which it was learned that just about every City fire code had been ignored or broken. It hadn't been arson but the D.A. filed charges against the building's owners as if they had lit a match. They copped a plea on a greatly reduced charge, ponied up enough money for a couple or ten college educations to make the case quietly go away. The same firm owned two other Center

City buildings and every time an alarm was struck firefighters hoped it was somewhere else.

"Let me be blunt. This kind of crime, and it's just as much a crime as a stick-up or drive-by shooting, is a reprehensible attack on the citizens of this city." Money cut. "We have to thank the weather that we can answer any questions this soon. The cold helped us get into the building much quicker than otherwise. The arson squad found evidence of an accelerant in three spots of the wreckage. I'm not going to say exactly what it was because of the nature of the investigation, but it was something that's readily available. John Q. Public can get a filler-up, but not many do. We calculate the loss here at close to five million dollars in the building and it'll take days or weeks to figure how to value the contents.

"We have to consider this the fire equivalent of a professional hit." Another money cut. "Sure, vandals set fires. It happens all the time, but usually with just one ignition spot and, even if the building goes up like this one did, we have a better chance to knock it down. We had no chance here. When the first ladder truck arrived, flames were visible in three spots along the south and west facings of the structure. The building was pre-sprinkler code so there was nothing we could do. Anyone who was there saw how close we came to losing men in the wall collapse.

"We have investigators following the money. This sort of crime is often financial and we expect to be able to find who benefits. Mayor."

Gilroy returned and said a few words about a neighborhood recovery center, aid for the nearest of neighbors whose homes were seared by the heat and how the Crime Commission had already put up a $10,000 reward for information. Maybe someone's memory could be jogged by such a jackpot.

He asked if there were any questions and the newspaper guys started in. Details on this, square-footage on that, who were the owners of the businesses, on and on. The party took about three times as long as it should have with all that lip-flap, and not one significant fact to show for it. I had what a needed, and more.

My attention wavered and I looked around. Watts was hunkered next to his cameraman like a guy awaiting the start of the Olympic hurdles. My spider sense tingled. You know what I mean. I was never bitten by a lab-altered spider but 15 years' experience that told me, don't skip out just yet.

The Mayor said, thanks, gotta run and was out the door followed by his security detail, bailing on Commissioner Bailey who was immediately surrounded by a phalanx of his top people. I looked at Watts who had lost one prey animal and was focused on Bailey like a lion in the bush. His cameraman disconnected from the mult-box and collapsed the tripod as Bailey, in the middle of a scrum, moved to the door.

I packed my gear into my bag and lurked. The Commissioner left room 202 and headed for the stairs, aiming for his car out on the concrete apron surrounding City Hall. Watts moved silently after him and while I was about to fall in line Sarah Tilson and her photographer suddenly joined the slow-speed chase. One of the newspaper reporters was oblivious, already typing pearls of prose on a net book, no doubt impressing the hell out of some editor, but the other seemed to realize something was up. College radio Annie was still trying to figure out if her recorder had worked.

I knew this game. Watts was onto something and he was angling for an exclusive. He probably had to act before the Commissioner got in his car (if Watts had access at another time we wouldn't have been playing fox and hounds) but when you grabbed a public official in a public place, you have to expect that other media types, nosey, paranoid media types, would listen in.

Watts saw he was screwed out an exclusive, but what could he do?

"Commissioner, I have another question for you." Bailey, about half out the City Hall door continued for another couple of steps so I thought for a moment he was blowing us off, but he was simply clearing the doorway. He turned.

"Yes, Mr. Watts, what is it?"

There was a moment's hesitation as cameras powered out of standby and microphones snapped to the ready.

"I have it on good authority that the accelerant used here was diesel fuel. Can you comment?"

For a flickering instant, Bailey looked as if he wanted to simply turn and get into the car, leaving the question to hang unanswered, but probably did a quick calculation: Garrison Watts knew people who told him on the QT what Bailey had not wanted to divulge upstairs. Watts could have waited and done a "sources tell me" on the early news, which would now be Plan B. But this barn was horseless and Bailey knew it.

"That is correct. Several gallons of diesel fuel were used as the accelerant in this fire. We know this because the arsonist left behind a gas can with a little bit of fuel left in it. Like a calling card. Weird. If he'd thrown it in the fire, we'd have been days looking for the cause. I wanted to keep this detail secret but, as long as it's not, I'll tell you we're working with trucking firms, gas stations and refineries in the area to see if we can find who bought it.." He paused for a second, then plowed on.

"Why don't we do this? Let's ask the public, right here, right now, to help us. This was a ten gallon gas can, and would have been awkward to carry when full, so maybe if someone in the neighborhood saw something out the window in the hours after midnight they can give the Crime Commission a call. This is just the kind of break we could use. Thank you."

This time he did make it into his car. His driver, a Fire Lieutenant, wheeled it around on the apron and took it out onto the street as the TV photographers grabbed video of the departure.

"Cool," said Sarah Tilson, tilting her head toward Watts.

"Fuck you," Watts said mildly. "Next time, get your own exclusive."

"Sharing time is a happy time," said Tilson, batting her eyes. I kept my mouth shut and headed for my car to file.

Chapter Five

It took me maybe 45 minutes to turn out one wrap and several voicecuts updating the fire story because I was getting brain-fried. I'd write, and then rewrite, and then re-rewrite. Now, there was even more information to cram in a report than before and since I'd been on the clock since 0:dark:30 the synapses were not cooperating.

Take one, take two, take three. Once I'd written the script, I couldn't deliver it. Thank God for the laptop because the story would be perfect by the time I transmitted it, but this was like pulling teeth out of my own mouth.

Finally, after I'd hit "send", I realized I hadn't eaten all day. That could have been a factor here. Low blood sugar.

Even in mid-winter, this end of the Parkway was alive with pedestrians at lunchtime, hustling here and there puffing clouds of breath like little locomotives. This wasn't my favorite section of town to catch a bite so I decided I could hold on for another half hour and called back to the station.

Silcox had gone home by then and Carrie Swoboda was the afternoon producer. I worked with her most days and we got along pretty well.

"Your updates are in the system," I told her. "It's arson and they have a reward out."

I heard computer keys clicking. "Okay, there it is. Hmm, diesel fuel. Someone was making a statement."

"Yeah, catch me. This whole thing strikes me as over the top. I don't know much about the arson business but it seems to me if you want to burn down your own building for the insurance or something you'd be more circumspect, you know, a gas or oil leak that meets a spark."

"Do we know who owns the building?"

"Not really. One of the newspaper guys asked but it's some real estate trust that no one's ever heard of. They'll have to follow a paper trail to find its owners and so on before they can even begin to check finances."

"Or just wait for the insurance claims to be filed."

"That'd work. Might not be aggressive enough. This was pretty damn reckless of whoever did it. They want him caught.

"Listen," I changed the subject, "I'm past the nine hour mark and I have to clock out. Are you going to be all right?"

"We're a little short with Gina out but we'll live. Nice job on this, by the way. This has legs for the rest of the day."

"Thanks. I'll see you tomorrow."

Tucking the phone in my coat pocket, I planned my afternoon. In order: food, nap, kids, wife.

I headed back up 95 to my guilty pleasure, a Chinese buffet near Franklin Mills Mall where I could feed my face in a hurry and catch up on my MSG.

Home was nearby, just across the city line in Benfranklin Township, in a townhouse complex north of Street Rd. That's right. The main drag in Benfranklin was called Street Rd. Not Road Rd., or Avenue Rd. or even Boulevard Rd., but Street Rd., and the most amazing thing was, no one seemed to think that was odd.

I lived in your standard-issue 3-bedroom townhome, the end of the row so it had a little more yard than most. Jen and I had talked about moving every time interest rates got low but if two kids were it for us there was no pressing need other than to acquire more stuff and more space to store it.

I hung up my coat, a concession to Jen who always fumed when I just tossed it on the couch, checked the phone for messages (one: an automated doctor's appointment reminder that was so annoying I wanted to cancel the damn thing) and stumbled upstairs to fall into bed.

I thought I'd fall asleep in a snap but details kept crowding in, mostly the nagging prospect of that deposition awaiting me in the morning like a no-anesthesia colonoscopy. Nevertheless, I did get a couple of hours Z's. By 4:00 I was puttering in the kitchen, half-listening to a talk show host butter up the latest author-friend, and setting up for the dinner that Jen had made ahead.

At 5, I got back in the car and headed to pick up the kids. It wasn't far, just into the city again. Over Poquessing and through the woods to grandmother's house we go. "Grandma" Betty Helms, my mother-in-law, was not exactly the bane of my existence but the kind of old nag I'd sometimes like to see headed to the glue factory.

We paid her to watch the kids during the week, which allowed Jen and me the freedom to work, but she charged a price that was sometimes higher than the money. It was the kind of "if you have them by the balls, their hearts and minds will follow" maternal realpolitik that left Jen and me constantly in her debt, constantly remembering that our lives were precariously balanced like a dime on a dashboard, waiting for Betty to swerve.

She lived in a modest rowhouse off Academy Road. The difference between a townhouse and a rowhouse was about $50,000 and maybe a few zip code digits. Hers began with 191, which meant Philadelphia, which meant it was worth considerably less than a few miles away in 190 country. 189 was even pricier but that was out in McMansion-land.

I squeezed into a parking space along the street and walked a couple of doors along the icy patchwork sidewalk to her stoop, still festooned with bedraggled evergreen boughs from Christmas. I jiggled the knob but it was locked so I rang the bell.

There was barking and squealing from inside as a dog and two children figured that company had arrived and all were sure it was just for them.

Betty answered the door shortly, looking a little disheveled. She had probably fallen asleep to the libidinous lullaby of the soaps. No, it wasn't the best grandparenting you could imagine but her house was pretty well childproofed by now. Everything breakable had been broken. Every outlet was capped, the stairs were gated, cabinets locked and there was some goofy device on the stove that meant you had to enter a code or sing a song or something to turn on a burner. It was a wonder the woman didn't starve to death.

Behind her, Doogie the doggie ran around in circles, threading in between two little girls whooping "Daddy, Daddy, Daddy!" It was a joyous greeting and just the kind of pick-me-up I needed.

"Howzit goin', Betty," I asked as I slipped past her into the bedlam. Doogie rolled over on his back, ready for a belly-rub, and the girls plowed into my legs like little linebackers. Doogie would have to wait. I stooped and scooped one kid in each arm. What a country!

Elizabeth was five with brown hair and hazel eyes but a sunny disposition that made her tough to resist. I'd had to take a pain pill more than once after being twisted around her little finger. Lorraine was three, blonde with baby blues and combative, mostly with big sister "Wizzy" but she could turn into a Dr. No that even James Bond couldn't beat.

I nuzzled each one and planted a big theatrical kiss on each forehead, drinking in their smells. This, I told myself every time, was why I put up with all the other bullshit, including Betty. Sure, she was doing us a favor by watching her granddaughters for a modest stipend but she never tired of reminding us of that, and demanding certain favors in return. Nothing smutty, of course. Betty was straight-laced Scots Presbyterian about most things, but I had spent an entire weekend installing her new water heater because it saved her some money. All I knew about plumbing is you push the handle and the poop goes somewhere else.

Well, it was a learning experience. Afterward, I felt entitled to show my butt crack any time I'm even near a tool belt.

"You hear about the storm coming in?" Betty asked. It was like smacking me across the face with a flounder.

"What storm?"

"You call yourself a reporter. It's been on all the shows." Of course, I call myself a reporter, I thought. I've been out reporting, not sitting on my ass dozing to the oldies....

"What do they say?"

"Tomorrow night into Wednesday. Six to eight inches."

This day just kept getting better and better. If I went out to the car now and turned on WPN or some other station or changed the TV to one of the local newscasts, it'd be the regular Chinese fire drill of pre-storm coverage. Its guidelines:

1) Fear and loathing, loathing and fear, oh my god we're all gonna die team coverage meteorologist live every two fucking minutes with the Electric Orbital Super-attenuated Ping Machine which can track a storm to your neighborhood, to your house, to your shower where it raises a knife!!!!!!

2) See guideline one.

I was amazed, actually, that it had taken so long. Storm hysteria is a staple of local media. It would be naive to suggest that the weather guy or gal come on and say, "Hey, folks, we'll be getting a little snow tomorrow night. It's winter in Philadelphia, after all. You might want to get up early and break out the shovel."

This weather system must have just formed because often they're now starting the snowstorm air raid siren five days or more before the big event. And if the storm you predict with such sound and fury doesn't occur, hey, look over here, a two-headed kitten, or blood on the street, could it happen here? (Well, it just did, nimrod) While doctors bury their mistakes, meteorologists are always looking five days ahead, not one behind.

This news changed what tomorrow looked like, and not for the better. Let's see: first, root canal, then proctoscopic. The deposition could last a couple of hours, then I'd have to finish off my workday with snow preparation duty. That meant touching the usual bases including PennDOT for its highway salting and clearing plans, SEPTA for its transit contingencies and the nearest supermarket to interview people buying milk, eggs and bread. When the going got tough around here, people made French toast.

Betty wasn't through with me yet.

"What's going on with you and Jen?" she asked after the kids ran off to collect their things.

"What are you talking about?" I was genuinely surprised by this line of interrogation. Browbeating me for not having a "real job", for "making her work" or for the catch-all crime of not being Betty's idea of the ideal son-in-law: those swipes were as common as dirt during my visits. But I thought things were fine with me and Jen, and I said so.

"Hmmph!" she snorted, sensing a cover-up. "When she arrived this morning, she looked like hell." And, of course, that must be my fault. "I called her at the shop about lunchtime, offered to make her some soup or something and she was abrupt, even rude, in giving me the bum's rush. Got customers, ma, gotta go. On a Monday in January, puh-lease."

"Maybe she's just not feeling well," I offered. "Look, I haven't seen or talked to her all day. I left the house in the middle of the night to cover a fire."

"Maybe the fire's in your home!" she snapped. "Your wife's upset or sick or got a stupid hang-nail and you don't know?" She made a dismissive just-like-a-man gesture and began to stomp off but turned, and a little softer said, "If it's anything I can help with, let me know."

"Thanks," I said, although it was sort of half-rage-choked with an unspoken you-ignorant-meddling-bitch chaser.

As I buckled the girls into their car seats a few minutes later, one part of my brain was hosting chit-chat about their day, which included an outing to the mall and the make-believe friends they shared from TV, while another was mapping out a way to find out if anything Betty said was true.

Jen wouldn't be home until later, her email had said, so she couldn't be that sick. She and I talked regularly and honestly, so I thought I was pretty current on her world. Sure, she had her problems at work, with Jan and, let's be honest, with me, but it wasn't anything worrying. Nonetheless, I was concerned.

Dinner, served microwave hot as soon as we got home, was meatloaf-a-roni, a nice kid-friendly meal to Elizabeth that Lorraine treated as if it were a puzzle to be solved. Tongue sticking out of her mouth in concentration, she'd pick an elbow macaroni there and a beef morsel there, admire it for a moment on her fork and only then eat it. Meals were marathons with Lorraine around. We used to have a rule that we all sat while we all ate dinner. Now, Jen was still at work or her meeting and I let Elizabeth slip off to play while Lorraine picked her dinner to death like the tide eroding a rock.

Eventually, we all cuddled on the couch to watch some "family-friendly" TV show that might have been just ducky for the Manson family but with potty jokes. Precocious, mouthy kids and preposterous plots wore out their welcome by the second thunderous news promo complete with its drumbeat of snow, Snow, SNOW! Live at 11!

I knew I wouldn't make it to the late news. Nap or no, I was beat and I was going to need some sleep to be clear-headed for the deposition. Best to get the young-uns to bed.

We started the ritual at 8:30 and still no Jen. Lorraine went to bed first. I carried her up the stairs, helped her with her toothbrush and changed her into her jammies before beginning the umpteenth identical adventure of The Very Hungry Caterpillar. She loved to wiggle her finger in the hole the caterpillar had "chewed" through the pages as we read them. I kissed her on the forehead and made a show of checking the closet for monsters, then began round two.

Go figure. Elizabeth, normally the cooperative one, dug in her heels.

"Not 'til Mommy's home," she pouted and while I could see her point this was a my-way-or-the-highway moment.

"Nope, bed time," and I scooped her up off the couch.

"No!" she cried pitifully. "Mommy!" I put her down gently and turned her to face me.

"We can do this the easy way or we can do this the hard way. Which do you want?" This was the standard refrain. The "easy way" was with hugs, kisses and a story. The "hard way" was a swat on the fanny and lots of yelling. Her choice. I was good either way.

Just then, there was a rattle at the front door and it pushed open revealing Jen, prying her key from the lock.

"Mommy!" squealed Elizabeth and I could hear Lorraine stirring upstairs. In a moment, she was giving us both a heart-attack by clambering down the stairs at wobbly full throttle. Jen made a good show of hugs and kisses while I stood aside. Oh, well, back to square one with beddy-bye time.

Jen looked drawn, pale, so maybe she was sick. You work in a two-person shop like she did, a sick day costs 50 percent of the work force. At age 35, she was still slim and could pass for her late 20's when the bags under her eyes weren't bigger than carry-ons at the airport.   She forced a smile through her full lips.

"Looks like I arrived just in time," she said as she disengaged from the girls.

"I was ready for the second round, coach. They never laid a glove on me." She put her coat away, looped her handbag strap over a hook in the wall and began shooing the kids upstairs.

"Oh, Mommy," Elizabeth whined, the "Oh" coming out of a major yawn. "I want to stay up with you."

"Me too!" put in little Miss "Me Too." Jen actually seemed to waver. There was a certain mistiness in her eyes as she looked from one to the other.

"No," I intervened to provide covering fire. "It's bedtime. Up, up, up the stairs," and I play-swatted two butts as they scurried away.

"Daddy's right," Jen jumped in. "Look at the time. Little girls need their sleep."

"But I'm a bigger girl," said Elizabeth. "I need less."

"'M'a bigger girl too," said Lorraine.

Jen sighed. She obviously had no stomach for a fight or a dustup or even a tiff, so I herded the girls, pleading, sniffling, whining, using every parent-distracting trick in their growing arsenals up the stairs. Lorraine got plunked right back in bed with another kiss from Dad and a special guest cuddle by Mom.

Elizabeth took more of a hand in her own evening ablutions and she read The Very Hungry Caterpillar to us, if you excused some adlibbing and just plain padding of the story to add a minute or so to the whole affair. Nevertheless, we kissed her goodnight and left Elizabeth cuddling Dr. Duck, a stuffed animal medical mallard that I'd brought back from a pediatricians' convention a few years before. Lorraine was already asleep.

I followed Jen into our bedroom where she began to change clothes. "Long day, huh?" I ventured, noncommittally. Jen would talk if she wanted. The third degree would avail me nothing.

"Mine? What about yours?" Already out of her shoes and slacks, she pulled off her blouse, a ribbed sleeveless turtleneck that never failed to get me aroused. "I heard you at the fire. That was a close call for the guys." Police were brothers, firefighters cousins, but it was all family. "What kind of a moron sets fire to a place like that, with homes so close? Whoever it is ought to be shot for recklessness alone!"

She slipped on a sweatshirt and sweatpants, completing the dowdy evening look with fuzzy slippers. Tres chic.

"Yeah, I'm kind of toasted. I got a nap but it's not enough." I wanted to keep it short and get the focus back on her.

"How was your meeting?"

She looked at me slightly puzzled. "Oh, the usual." She slipped past me and headed down to the kitchen. I followed, mute. She scooped a little room-temperature dinner-aroni into a dish and set the microwave to warming it. She went to the liquor cabinet, grabbed the bourbon and poured herself a shot and a half by my eyeball measurement. No sooner than she had plunked a couple of ice cubes in it than the microwave announced it was done.

She delivered glass, dish and fork to a bistro table in the corner, too high as yet for the kids, and sat down.

"You want something?" she asked after a mouthful.

"A little conversation would be nice."

"I don't feel much like talking. It's been a long and exhausting day."

"Trouble at the mill? Flay-rod gone out-of-skew on treadle?" Usually an obscure line from Monty Python would at least bring a smile. No such luck this time.

"What part of "I don't feel much like talking" don't you understand?"

Stung, I backed off. Fine, I may not be the most perceptive guy in the room (even when I'm the only guy in the room) but you don't need to hit me with a 2x4 all that often.

I flopped on the couch in the family room, remote in hand, and clicked through the cable channels. Shit, crap, feces, poop, tripe, garbage, retread, the half-vast wasteland of television lay before me like a big valley in Utah where explorers discovered the central lake was salt water. It was a bitter pill paying so much money a month for hundreds of channels of nose-picking drivel.

I finally settled on a Law and Order re-run ripped from the headlines of a gentler time when such a crime was actually considered unusual.

Jen finished eating and cleaned up silently. The noise from the TV was our ears' only companion. I looked over at her as she poured herself a second hefty bourbon. The bad news, said the angel on one shoulder, is that she usually didn't drink much and maybe she was upset about something. The good news, said the devil on the other shoulder, is maybe you're about to get lucky.

She eased down next to me on the couch, ice cubes jingling, breasts jiggling. I sure hoped that little devil was right.

"Sorry," she offered without explanation. "Jan and I are having a time of it."

I put my arm around her and pulled her close. She hugged her drink but didn't push me away.

"I have to give a deposition first thing in the morning," I mentioned as casually as possible.

"What on earth for?" I explained the situation, from Warren Peter Nash's probable nefarious activities which I could only suspect, to Agent Semyenovic's two-fer, getting to Nash through me and, if not, getting to me anyway.

"Cops think they can get away with anything," she huffed. I was startled. That was quite an admission (albeit often true) from her.

"What makes you say that?"

She didn't answer for a moment, then looked at me with eyes narrow. "I deal with them all the time. My sister is married to one." Duh.... "Look, it's been a trying day for both of us. Maybe we just ought to go to bed."

I was about to make an issue of it but she put down her glass and swiveled toward me. She leaned in gently and planted a long, lingering, delightful kiss on me. I responded and we clung together necking for some time.

"Maybe we ought to go to bed," she whispered throatily, and the little devil did a victory dance.

45

Chapter Six:
Tuesday

The next morning, my body was up-and-at-'em long before my mind, which I think was averting its gaze from the coming day. The first thing I remember was gouging myself during the male ritual self-sacrifice known as shaving. A toilet-paper bandage finally got the bleeding to stop but as omens went I hardly needed someone with a phony Eastern European accent to interpret it.

Somehow miraculously dressed, I ran into Jen in the kitchen as she made breakfast for Elizabeth who was as chirpy as a chickadee. I gave them both a peck and plowed into the fridge looking for my caffeine fix. Coffee was not my vice but a diet cola put fizz in my day. We were almost out. I grabbed the last Coke One and tried to hide it but Eagle-eye Elizabeth spotted me.

"No soda for breakfast!" she parroted. "No soda for breakfast!"

Jen gave me a look but didn't say anything. The rule, after all, was for the kids but with me providing such a bad example every day it was sometimes a chore to enforce. I grabbed a bowl of cereal and the milk and was in mid-crunch when Lorraine walked in yawning and stretching like someone in a mattress commercial.

"M'hungry," she said and climbed up into her chair.

"Do you want eggs or cereal?" Jen asked.

"Donuts," said Lorraine. Child psychologists tell you to limit kids' choices. Kids have other ideas.

"We don't have any donuts. You can have cereal or eggs."

Lorraine settled for a bowl of some marshmallow-based junk that reeked of sugar and cavities to come. But she dived right in and voiced no complaints. Be thankful for small favors.

I checked the clock. "Gotta go," I said, stopping to kiss each of my girls.

"You're not going to wear a tie?" Jen asked/criticized.

"No." I replied. "If they're going to hang me, they'll have to provide the noose."

I hated neckties. The damn things choke off the blood flow to the head, which explains a lot about the state of the world when you consider how many of the high and mighty wear them. I also considered them penises, the phallic display that men didn't have the courage to actually make, so they hung this cloth dick around their necks as a totem of sexual prowess. If ties weren't penises, then how come wearing a tiny bow tie, which strangles you just as well as any Windsor knot, is seen as less masculine?

"Wish me luck. Deposition early, probably some road warrior duty later. I don't know when I'll be home."

"Mom's good," Jen smiled with a little bit of wistful warmth. "She already has the makings of French toast." Jen walked me to the door and gave me a bigger hug and wetter kiss than I'm used to. "I just want to say good luck. We're all counting on you." Good, an "Airplane!" reference. Now that was my Jen.

I got into the morning conga line on 95 and listened to a couple of news cycles on various stations. You could even grab the audio from one of the TV morning shows on one of the HD radio bands but I wasn't that desperate and settled for an audio dissertation on African tribal masks on NPR.

Take Two, A Smart-ass Mystery

The main local headline was, of course, the snow. No, pardon me, THE SNOW! It was discussed with such forthright urgency that you'd have thought I was in Miami facing down Blizzard Andrew. You know, a few years back, one of the TV news shows actually tried naming winter storms like hurricanes, an idea that blessedly starved to death at a young age.

Parking was going to be an issue. The FBI office sat right off Independence Mall, close to the Federal Courthouse, and across the street from a Federal prison, creating this nice Tinker-to-Evers-to-Chance rock-'em-sock-'em law enforcement combination. There was an underground lot that cost as much as an airline ticket and a couple of hotel garages but with on-street parking so scarce, thousands of people came in on the bus, subway or train. I didn't really have that option since, barring my arrest during the deposition, I would have work to do elsewhere.

I got off 95 at the eastern Center City ramp and twisted through a couple of narrow colonial era streets that were all marked, two hour parking. Did I feel lucky? What the hell, Nash wouldn't dare deny paying my ticket, given what I was there for.

Walking to the FBI Building, I passed Philadelphia's fortresses of money, the Mint where they made it and the Federal Reserve where they stepped on its neck and told it to hold still. Both were gated and buff like WWE wrestlers made of concrete. The Mint had a delivery door that I swear was pilfered from the Death Star at a salvage sale.

I passed through Federal security with no hassles and made my way up to the appointed floor. Neither way out of elevator lobby seemed to be right. There was nothing labeled "FBI", "Federal depositions here" or "Casting call for Bubba's jailhouse squeeze." I slipped past one glass partition into a waiting room where a woman behind a slab of bank-teller glass managed to ignore me for a full minute.

"Hi," I rapped a knuckle on the glass. "Am I in the right place for a federal deposition?"

"What's your name?" She clicked at a computer keyboard.

"Bernie Gaston. G-A-S-T-O-N."

"Ah, yes Mr. Gas-tone. Do you have counsel?"

I looked around the empty room. "I'm supposed to have a lawyer."

"Who is it?" She raised her purple-nailed fingers to type the name.

"I don't know," I was embarrassed to say. I had given Lorne two names but gotten no confirmations.

She looked at me for a moment and I could hear her smacking gum. She wore an expression behind which I would imagine slaughterhouse workers hide as they hustle unsuspecting animals down their final chute. "Well, I'll let Agent Semyenovic know you are here."

I whipped out my cell phone and called the station. Maybe Nash was in or even Lorne. God knows, I was that desperate, but the line clicked over to voicemail hell. I punched in Nash's extension and got more voicemail.

"Mr. Nash. Warren. This is Bernie Gaston. I'm at my deposition, alone! Where's my lawyer?"

"Problem? " came a voice behind me. I spun and there stood Special Agent Gary Semyenovic who, if he'd been a beat cop, would have been smacking a nightstick in his hand for emphasis. His eyes came in a pretty close second.

"Yeah," I snapped the phone closed. "No lawyer."

"No problem." Suddenly, Agent Semyenovic was all used-car-salesman. We were best buddies. He shouldn't do this and his boss would probably kill him but here's an offer you can't refuse. "We can wait a few minutes but you know this is really nothing to worry about. Just a few routine questions."

I looked at my watch. 9:05. "My lawyer....."

"Is probably just caught in traffic. We can start and he can catch up."

"Well...."

"Then you can get on with the rest of your day. I'm sure you have things to do, what with the incoming storm."

"Ten minutes," I managed. "Give me ten minutes."

"Fine." Agent Semyenovic, resplendent in a dark pinstriped suit with a light blue shirt and a dark blue dick, er, tie, backed off like a funeral director who knew that no one, much less the guest of honor, was leaving.

I knew what an insect trapped in a web felt like when the spider dallied.

I called the WPN main number two more times and then the newsroom. Silcox answered. "Where are you?"

"The deposition. Remember the memo we all got? I'm an appetizer! Nash is the main course! Have you seen him or Lorne?"

"No, but they never come back here. You know that."

I was really getting a tension headache, like the lead-off batter in World Series game 7. It wasn't all on me but I was the first one it was on.

"Look, if you see them, tell them I have NO LAWYER HERE!" I didn't mean to yell, really, but receptionist went all librarian on me.

Ten minutes vanished like money from my budget and Agent Semyenovic ushered me into a nondescript room with a window overlooking Independence Mall. There was a stenographer and another man who introduced himself as a forensic accountant on the other side of the conference table from me. Semyenovic leaned genially on its end.

We started off easy, like the first few moments as a roller coaster is cranking you up gently into the sky and you're looking around saying, this isn't so bad. I can see my house from here and then....

Sworn-in, I answered their questions beginning with name, rank and serial number, well, social security. They wanted my job history at WPN so they got a mini-resume.

What was my relationship with Mr. Nash? Yesterday, when he told me I had to be deposed was the first time I'd talked to him in a couple of weeks.

"You're saying you have no day-to-day contact with him? He does not micromanage?" Semyenovic asked. The other guy just stared.

"He doesn't micromanage me. He has little contact with the newsroom."

"That's strange." Semyenovic rustled through some papers on his desk. "You did a story yesterday on skiing this weekend."

"Yes."

"And who did you interview?"

I had to think back. It was only yesterday but I hadn't paid much attention to that thumbsucker when I did it. "Charles Van-der-something. Van Dros, General Manager of White Mountain Ski Resort."

"Did Mr. Nash or any of his subordinates tell you to call that resort?"

"No!" It was ridiculous to even suggest. Nash never interfered. "I went online, Googled and grabbed. It was real quick and dirty."

Semyenovic raised an eyebrow. "Quick and dirty?"

"Get in, get out, move on. It's like the radio reporter's creed."

"So you're saying, under oath, that no one told you to call White Mountain?"

Warning! Warning! Danger, Will Robinson! "What do you mean? Someone did tell me to do a story on skiing but not to call White Mountain or any particular place. Just get some sound, put it on the radio, that's all."

"That's interesting," he said, slipping in front of me the piece of paper that he'd been tickling. "What is this?"

I gave it a quick scan and my eyes just about jumped out of my head. Although I had almost never seen one of them, it was a commercial order form on WPN stationary with instructions to the traffic department, the ones that placed spots, not reported on gridlock, to schedule a new sponsor, White Mountain Ski Resort. Although the document was dated last week, the start-date for the commercial run was tomorrow.

I gagged when I started to speak. You didn't have to be a forensic accountant or a suspicious, revenge-minded Federal agent to see how this looked. It looked like payola, that to sweeten the deal for commercials White Mountain was paying for, we gave them a "news story" commercial off the books.

"You see my problem," Agent Semyenovic leaned in. He really could have used a breath mint. "Did Mr.Nash or any of his subordinates tell you to call this ski resort to do your story?"

"No," I managed. "This is the first I've heard of the spot order. Before yesterday I'd never even heard of White Mountain. I don't ski." I revisited the moment when I chose White Mountain. No one had suggested it! I wouldn't have made the call if I'd known about this.

"Once again, Mr. Gaston, may I remind you that you are under oath. You are saying that these two facts, that you interviewed the General Manager of the White Mountain Ski Resort and put him on the air yesterday talking about this weekend's skiing, and that that same General Manager at that same ski resort is the source of this" he waved the paper "several thousand dollar commercial order, you are saying this is a coincidence? A very happy and profitable coincidence?"

"Yes," I rasped. "That's all it is." I wasn't so sure I believed it myself.

There was a long silence, which I half expected to be broken by the rattle of handcuffs being slapped on me, or the drone of my Miranda rights being read.

Agent Semyenovic decided to take a potty break. I went over to the window and tried my cell phone lifeline. Still no answer at the station, just the maddening recorded message. I punched Nash's extension and got his voicemail too. What the hell was going on? Everyone taking an early snow day?

I dropped the phone back in my pocket and sighed. My stress headache could now chew through rebar.

The interview resumed shortly with Semyenovic seeming to have retreated from his accusatory demeanor, but I was wary. He paced around the small room like a bull sure there must be another red flag to charge. Soon, after tedious softball questions about my job, my colleagues, my boss and all sorts of other crap that wouldn't interest my most demented fan, or my mother, God rest her soul, he made his move.

"What do you know about the Rosen-Philadelphia Real Estate Investment Trust?"

"Never heard of it," I responded quickly, and only then began wondering if I actually had. REITs were a blessing and a curse in Philadelphia. They were responsible for moving some neighborhoods from life-support into desirability, but while their investors made money the longtime residents could find themselves re-assessed out of their homes. It's an old and on-going story and so not often news.

"Really?" he replied, and I could sense another pounce coming. "Because the Rosen-Philadelphia REIT owns that building that burned down yesterday morning, the diesel fuel arson job that you covered." He paused and I felt that I was expected to say something, but I hadn't been asked a question. He fiddled with the stack of papers on the table again and handed one to me. "Recognize any of these investors?"

It was a long list, but alphabetized, and there among the N's was Nash, Warren Peter. I gulped down my surprise, pretending to read the rest of the names.

"Well, I certainly recognize a few but I guess you're going for my boss, Mr. Nash."

"Were you aware of his financial involvement with this arson?"

"Now, wait a minute!" I responded sharply. "That's a bit of a leap. Even if this is a current investors list, accurate right up to this morning, there's nothing to indicate Mr. Nash or any of these people burned their own investment!"

"That's the good little soldier," he responded, smiling slyly, producing two more papers. "This," he said, wiggling one, "is the City's tax assessment of that fire trap, half a million dollars, and I think they were being generous. This," as he jiggled the other sheet, "is the declarations page of an insurance policy. I draw your attention to the insured amount. Fifteen million dollars."

"Whoa!" I blurted. The Fire Lt. had said five mil. These numbers were all over the map.

"You see my point," he continued pleasantly. "You see how this looks."

"It looks as if it's still an unsolved arson, although now we know there's plenty of financial gain."

"What does your boss know about this?"

"Ask him."

"I will, but you're here now. You claim to know nothing about the business end of your own business..."

"I don't! Not much, anyway."

"And you sit here under oath, copping that I-know-nothing, I-see-nothing attitude. You work for a criminal! Your money is dirty! You are dirty!" He slammed his palm down on the table with such force that the transcriptionist jumped in her seat. The accountant checked his watch.

I sat back and watched Semyenovic go red in the face. This guy was seriously in need of a chill pill.

In a moment, I'd made a decision. "Listen, this has been a blast, but I think we're done here." I stood up slowly and turned toward the door, waiting for him to yell, or protest or cock a gun. I put my hand on the doorknob and turned back to give him a final glance. He sat on the edge of the table, fists clenched, staring hard at something only he could see.

I slipped out of the building uneventfully, but expecting at any moment I would suddenly be surrounded by FBI vehicles lurching up on the curb, and agents springing out with guns drawn.

That didn't happen, but my car did have two parking tickets on it.

Chapter Seven

I should have called in to the newsroom to tell them I was available but I was just too pissed off. As I drove out to the station I might as well have had my eyes closed, for all I was paying attention. Somehow I ended up in the parking lot, dodging potholes and trucks, and finally coming to a crooked stop in a puddle.

My little angel was whispering for calm, uttering cautionary reminders about rash actions ruining careers and tiny mouths at home that needed food, but the little devil was in full shout with the voice of 20,000 Flyers fans during a hockey fight, a roaring red spot of rage that was just looking for someone to take it out on.

I stomped past the newsroom and if anyone saw me they didn't say, out into the station lobby where fuck-head Lorne was curled up whispering on the phone again and TBC's office door was open. I stopped, confused by a target-rich environment but my momentary paralysis ended when Lorne looked up and said, "You're late. Where have you been?"

Blood boiled, volcanoes erupted, black and white footage of A-bomb tests blew houses apart as I yelled back, "Where have I been! I have been being grilled by the fucking FBI! And without a fucking lawyer! Where was my fucking lawyer?"

I was about six inches from Lorne's butt-fat face when light dawned on it. "I guess I forgot," he shrugged. "Whoops..."

My fist caught him in his blubbery cheek and spilled him over backwards from his chair. His shriek and the clatter of tumbling furniture brought several people into the lobby, Nash among them.

"What the hell is going on here?" he roared as I shuddered in fury and Lorne weepily tried to untangled himself. "Bernie, have you gone insane?"

I wheeled on him. "Insane? No, I'm stone-cold rational," I lied. "I've just spent two hours being grilled by an FBI agent who's after your ass, about your activities and without, without! benefit of the lawyer you said you'd provide to protect us both!"

"What did you tell him?"

"Oh, get a grip. I don't know anything about your activities, but you left me hanging out there with a big fat "kick me" sign on my ass and Agent Semyenovic teed me up again and again. That guy is after you, Warren. He's got his sights set on you."

By rights, I should have been fired on the spot. Insubordination and assault would make a tidy one-two combination, but instead TBC looked over at Lorne, who had climbed quivering to his feet. "I told you to make sure he had a lawyer."

"I..."

"This is my ass on the line here, you little shit. My company, my money!"

"I forgot."

"Forgot? Too busy having phone sex with your faggoty friends? Son of a bitch!"

"But Uncle Warren, he hit me!"

The temperature in the room dropped by about 100 degrees. Nash looked at his nephew with undisguised contempt, a decision made. "Get out," he said calmly.

"But Uncle Warren...."

"Get out or I swear I will hit you myself, you stupid, immature, lazy piece of trash." Nash moved toward Lorne like a boxer just daring a fallen foe to rise. Lorne backed away, swiping for his coat which lay tossed on the floor from his tumble. "Out!" Nash bellowed, pointing imperiously, and Lorne scuttled through the front door.

Nash turned to me. "In my office, now!" in a tone that brooked no hesitation.

I entered and sat. He shut the door and walked to his desk. "I'm really sorry about this," he said, surprisingly calmly. "I should have gotten rid of him years ago. I can already hear the call from my sister, but this time I'm not taking him back. The agent, what's he looking for?"

"Mostly, he was fishing but there is one thing. The Rosen-Philadelphia Real Estate Investment Trust."

I paused, awaiting a reaction but the only one I got was, "Is that supposed to mean something to me?"

"He showed me papers that you're an investor in it, and it owns and has suspiciously over-insured that building that was torched yesterday morning."

"Hmm," was all Nash managed but he seemed more perplexed than upset.

"Are you an investor in this thing?"

He shrugged. "Could be. I have money stashed, invested, all over the place. I'll check with my accountant. But that's it? That's it?"

"He tried to make something of my doing an interview with a ski mountain that the station is about to advertise but there was nothing to it. I called them out of the blue, didn't even know they were becoming a client."

"The fire at the warehouse, huh?" He seemed not to be listening to me, but wondering if the law could tag him with the arson. "Okay," he resumed after a moment's thought. "I've been down this deposition road before. You'll get a transcript in a few days that you're supposed to go over for accuracy. Make sure I get a copy. Now, get out of here."

"So, am I fired?" My stomach tumbled as I asked.

"No, get back to work, but no more hitting people, even if they really, really deserve it."

My first stop was the washroom where I splashed some cold water on my face and took a look at myself in the mirror. This is what a man who just dodged a cannonball looks like, maybe two cannonballs.

One thing was sure, this day could only go uphill from here.

Chapter Eight

I got a few odd looks in the newsroom from people who must have poked their heads out into the lobby during my meltdown, but I picked up an assignment, the traditional PennDOT storm preparation story, and off we went.

Greeting a storm is a finely honed routine in Philadelphia media. There are extra sessions with the meteorologist who will say over and over and over that it's going to snow. Someone will be live at the salt depot, someone else at the Home Depot and reporters donning their best gravitas and muk luks will be all over the place proving that it really will snow in Philadelphia in January.

Well, a PennDOT spokesman was Johnny-on-the-spot with all the details, a breakdown of the brine solution they'll squirt first from their plow trucks to prevent the early flakes from sticking, and then take off the gloves to pour ton after ton of salt crystals on state highways as things really get going, and finally lower the plows as the accumulation increased.

Snip, snip, write, write, and before you could say Bernie the snowman I had a couple of stories on the air so it looked like I was doing something more than dodging questions and pummeling receptionists.

Carrie Swoboda was the producer by then and Hank O'Hare (I swear I'm not making this up) the anchor. O'Hare was this old goat from the old school, the school where radio anchors just filled the time and didn't get involved with actually writing anything. He would pull copy off the wire, stuff written in newspaper inverted pyramid style, and read it cold on the air. It was an amazingly news-like experience. It should mean something, given his stentorian tone, but at the end all you'd be saying is, "Huh?"

O'Hare would sit in the studio for six hours a day, studying for his News as a Foreign Language exam, and surfing porn sites. Carrie would email him his line-up and his scripts and he would mumble them into the microphone right on cue. If ever interrupted from this routine, he would spill forth with such a string of profanity, character assassination and descriptions of impossible sexual positions that truck drivers at the warehouse would demand earplugs. Sure, with all the anti-sexual harassment laws and whatnot, Carrie could have gotten him fired in about two seconds, but as long as you understood the drill Hank was low maintenance and that left her plenty of time for eBay.

I volunteered to go for lunch at a pizzeria down the road in Conshohocken, which was an old riverside mill town that was in some sort of post-post-industrial revival with condos, latte bars and the mandatory Starbucks on every corner.

Carmine's Pizza was a throwback, the sort of greasy spoon that the health department avoided citing as a waste of paper. The owner was Frank Sterling but with his sauce-smeared apron and hair tucked into a stupid looking white cap he played the part of "Carmine" to a T. There was supposed to be no smoking in the restaurant but that was only enforced up front. The kitchen was thick with tobacco fumes, which added a certain something to the large pies, one pepperoni, one sausage and peppers, that I was to pick up.

"They say we're in for a storm," said Frank. As he worked the register, there was a TV on behind him where "they" were saying it quite often, with satellite images and Doppler and the ping machine all jiggering up the urgency.

"Yeah, it's going to snow."

"They're saying maybe 8 inches by morning."

"I'll let you know. I'll probably be out driving in it half the night."

"Anybody smart would stay home," he said, tossing a few breadsticks into a bag. Just what we needed, more carbs.

"Anybody smart wouldn't work at WPN," I replied. I didn't elaborate on how my day was going. He wasn't my barber or bartender.

But a couple of minutes later, while driving back to the station, against my better judgment I tuned us in. I usually don't. It was too annoying to hear how good news goes bad when passed through the Hank filter, but there he was pontificating about the incoming storm. Our weather service, which seemed to be three college kids with a computer, was predicting six to eight inches beginning as sleet in the evening rush. Oh, fucking, boy. That meant live shots from this highway and that for at least four hours on top of what had already been exhausting. I'm not the greatest driver in snow and Jen often threatens to tie me to the bumper if I don't calm the hell down. But she didn't spend three hours in a frozen ditch when she was a kid, in those pre-cell phone days when being stuck in the middle of nowhere actually meant something.

I finally hit the road about 3 p.m. and did my first live-shot at 3:31 wherein I informed our audience, no doubt breathless with anticipation and hanging on my every word, that things were just fine on the Blue Route, except for all the people driving like assholes. In so many words, of course.

The Blue Route, or I-476, was sort of Philadelphia's western beltway, connecting I-95 south of town with the Schuylkill Expressway and then the Pennsylvania Turnpike at the massive Mid-County Interchange. It was one of the bellwethers for a storm like this, which is likely to get worse first west of the city. This is due to elevation, distance from the coast, the approach track of the storm and all sorts of meteorology shit that the TV talking heads blather on about for hours.

For my next live shot, I swung around at an interchange and headed further west to Route 202, which ran through the high tech neighborhood around King of Prussia. Still no snow but plenty of flakes, drivers who we in the media had successfully panicked into racing like it was a videogame where tickets are never issued and crashes don't count.

By 5:30, and way the heck out the Pottstown Expressway, I was seeing sleet. Boop, boop, boop, this just in. The end of the world has begun in Limerick. More after this word from our sponsor.

I was eastbound on the highway where there was less traffic on my side, but a never-ending ribbon of headlights coming the other way. I wasn't paying much attention to them, being busy as I was trying to stay out of the trunk of the guy in front of me, but something caught my eye off to the left. Two westbound headlights swerved but didn't stop in the inner lane. They kept on going, the vehicle, a mid-size SUV, catching some low-beam illumination as it hit the left shoulder and then some low guide wires before rolling over them into the grassy median.

Taillights on my side erupted as drivers began to notice the commotion. The SUV tumbled into the depression that separated the opposing lanes of traffic, and ended up on its side. Suddenly the highway was like whitewater rafting for 100 cars. They were going this way and that, braking, steering, accelerating, trying to find a gap and get away, or maybe a place to stop.

Strangling the wheel, I ended up over on the shore of the median with traffic lurching past. I keyed in 911 and reported the crash to State Police, then put on my flashers and headed for the wreck. The SUV was lying on its driver side, wheels pointing toward the late lamented highway with no sign of movement within. A couple of other vehicles had pulled off the westbound side and brave souls were approaching it, trying not to fall down on the slick grass.

For a sickening moment, there was no movement from the SUV, but as we got close and a siren sounded in the distance, the passenger-side door first fluttered, then burst open and a disheveled woman stuck her head out.

"Help me!" she yelled. "My baby...."

We rescuers clambered near. Someone hauled her out and a couple of us braced a guy up on the side panel to grab the rear door and open it. The piercing wail of scared-to-death kid was our reward. The guy on the car lay down behind the passenger door and reached into the darkness. A moment's fumbling with a car seat latch later and he hauled himself out with baby on board. The little one was handed to mom who was blubbering like a kid with a splinter.

Only then did it occur to me to look at my watch. 6:01. Late. I speed-dialed the station and a curt Carrie connected me to the studio. Hank had been replaced by Gina Ginelli, who took the last second add in stride.

"WPN's Bernie Gaston is live with us from, from where? What are you seeing?"

"I'm in the median of Route 422 past Limerick where just moments ago an SUV careened off the westbound lanes and overturned. Brave motorists helped a mom and her baby out of the car and they seem more shaken than injured. But, folks, this stuff is sticking. It is slicking up this major road, so the minor ones may be even worse. Let's make it home in one piece, shall we? Live on Route 422, Bernie Gaston, WPN News."

I heard Gina pick up the rest of the newscast, and Carrie came back on the line. "Get some sound," she said. "See you at 6:30."

Getting the interviews was a snap. People babble during crises. I had Mom and several of the good Samaritans before the State Police got close. To avoid time-consuming bureaucratic entanglements, I slipped back across the median and eased my car into eastbound traffic that was at a rubberneck crawl past the crash scene.

Over the next two hours and four more live shots, travel got worse and worse. In fact, the forecasters were changing gears faster than a NASCAR driver, trying to keep up with the changing outlook. More here, less there, ice in the middle.

There were a couple of times when I thought I'd be going ditch diving. Traction was miserable on some of the major non-expressway roads, a situation made worse by the terrain north and west of Philly. Hills and trees sure were pretty most of the time but in zero visibility, with my headlights reflecting back from snow streaming past like a Star Wars hyperspace jump, it was bad. And on a winding road that some nimrod decorated with state route markers even though it was just a two-lane paved cow path uncluttered by street lamps and lined by thick tree trunks that whipped past like bridge abutments, I wanted nothing more than to park in front of my own house. My knuckles were as white as the KKK's laundry.

I was heading back up Route 202, where travel had been reduced to one lane and we all drove in the tire tracks of the next guy in line, when my phone rang. I know I'm not supposed to be yakking and driving one-handed in a blizzard, but pulling over was simply out of the question.

"This is Bernie," I answered, expecting it to be the station.

"BG, it's me." Jen. "Something's happened."

"What? Are you all right?"

"Yeah, I'm fine. No, I'm not. It's Frank. He's dead."

"What?" Frank wasn't my favorite guy but, since he was a cop, I always knew a phone call like this was a possibility. "What happened?"

There was a long pause. "Jan shot him."

If I had been stunned before, this was like catching a wooden beam across the beak. My keen reporter's instincts kicked in and I managed, "Huh, what, how?"

"Not now," said Jen, tearful. "Get over to their house. I'll meet you there after Mom gets here to watch the kids." The line went dead and I drove along on autopilot. I was halfway down the Turnpike to the Northeast before I called the newsroom to sign out for the night. I didn't say why.

Chapter Nine

Frank and Jan's house was off the Boulevard, near a vast tract that used to be a mental hospital. It was maybe 10 minutes from my house and five minutes from the Turnpike but that night it might as well have been on the moon. While PennDOT took care of most state roads, and every Philadelphia trash truck was outfitted with a plow for tonight's festivities, the Turnpike had its own crews and they must have been busy elsewhere because there would have been white-out conditions, if there'd been enough light. I listened to some traffic updates and things were so bad it was shorter to list where the roads were not a mess.

I probably did 35 in a 65 zone all the way from King of Prussia to the Benfranklin Interchange. My nerves had nearly gotten the better of me when some moron in a Beamer shot past at Warp Factor One, leaving a rooster tail of slush that bitch-slapped the left side of my car and poured a dirty smear on the windshield. I fought to go straight while the wipers struggled. A few miles later, the same guy was off on the shoulder, 180 degrees turned to traffic. I resisted the urge to call it in. When I finally eased up the ramp to southbound Route 1 about 9:20, I felt I'd gone a few rounds with the champ.

US 1 ran from Maine to Florida and was a mixed bag of everything from expressway to city street to country road but for the most-part in Philadelphia it was "The Boulevard." Sure, the city had other boulevards, JFK and Lindbergh to name two, but if you ask, "Which way to the Boulevard?" no one will direct you any place but this. Route 1 is four lanes north of the Turnpike, six lanes for about a mile to its south where it crosses the city line and balloons into Roosevelt Boulevard, a highway monstrosity left over from long ago. Twelve lanes of traffic in four three-lane sections, with cross-streets, crossovers, turn lanes and even the occasional under- or over-pass. It's a freeway built by traffic light salesmen and body shop operators. Two intersections along it were constantly on the insurance industry's list of the most dangerous in the country.

Tonight, as I hit the free-for-all zone where Route 1 expands into the Boulevard like Bruce Banner into the Hulk, and drivers usually career left and right trying to find their new lane, its only saving grace was almost nobody was out. I saw only a few head and tail lights as I approached Southampton Road where I ducked off into the neighborhood.

This was a little bit of suburbia in the city, with neat rowhouses on a few blocks interspersed with single family homes, some dating back to when this was a bucolic outpost surrounded by farmland. It looked like a Christmas card, all quiet and snowy, lit by the orange glow of streetlamps, until I turned onto Jan and Frank's street.

I didn't get far before a police cruiser, its roof lights dancing blue and red, blocked the road. I could see TV live-trucks ahead but my car wasn't painted all over with station logos, so I parked and hoofed it. Since I'd begun the day at an FBI inquisition, all right, deposition, and the storm had then seemed far, far away, I didn't have my boots and my shoes were coated with snow and slush by the time I got close.

Their house, a ramshackle clapboard two-story affair with a detached garage on an alley out back, was lit up like the Linc at game time. The cops aimed some car and wagon headlights, and the TV trucks, four of them, had rows of lamps along each roofline so the place was brighter than noon, that day anyway. A couple of photographers were shivering in the storm, awaiting any miniscule morsel of video that might tell the story, while their reporters sat toasty in the vans.

I tried to avoid them. This was awful enough without having to dodge questions for which I had no good answers. I started to cut up the lawn, when a cop yelled, "Hey! Get off!"

That got the photogs attention but most of them knew me from WPN so they didn't shoot, figuring I was about to join the quarantine. The first rule of police work was, control the media. The second was, use the media.

"You can't go in there. It's a crime scene," said the cop.

"I'm family," I said quietly so as not to wake the sleeping camera hounds. "Frank's my brother-in-law."

"You wait here," replied the officer and he turned toward the house, walking across the lawn following the only set of tracks in the still-falling snow. He opened the storm door and the inner door and said something to silhouettes I could now see inside. "Come on," he waved me up.

As I reused the one line of footprints through the snow, there were stirrings behind me as the photogs took cameras off standby to catch what little was happening.

"Hey," called a voice I recognized as Garrison Watts. "Hey, Bernie!" But I was in the house before I heard the rest.

As the door sighed shut behind me, it was as if I'd fallen down Lewis Carroll's rabbit hole into a place where nothing made sense. To my right was the family room, where Jen cuddled with my 5-year-old niece Samantha and her younger brother 2 year old Frank junior. If it weren't my wife with their kids in their house, it would have been lovely, except that everyone was crying. They hadn't even noticed me.

To my left in the living room, was, as they say, the scene of the crime. Living room, my eye. Two police evidence technicians stood over Frank who lay spread-eagle on the floor. He was wearing grimy sweat pants and a hoodie that had two big red holes in it, about mid-chest. He was staring at the ceiling. There was some blood spatter on a knee wall behind him and probably some in the dining room beyond but I couldn't see it.

In the corner to my left, Jan sat in an overstuffed chair, looking very small, kind of turned in on herself. Her right arm was across her chest supporting the left, which was tucked into a sling. The spot was unusually dark and it took me a moment to figure out why. A lamp, battered and broken, lay in a heap in the corner a few feet from its usual post on an end table. Two detectives loomed over her, questioning her in hushed tones.

One turned to me, gave me a brief look, then did a double-take.

"Fuck, who let you in? I'll arrest your ass, posing as family." It was Homicide Captain C.J. Pell, with whom I had interacted/tangled on a few occasions.

Clarence Johnston Pell was in his mid-50's, a burly fireplug of a man with graying sandy hair cut in police buzz and a brush moustache that seemed to stiffen his upper lip. He and Detective Jim Dellacourt, his taller younger partner, traveled in a pack, with Pell the alpha male. I knew from experience that you never called him Clarence and even "C.J." was taking a chance.

"My bad," said Dellacourt.

"I am family. Brother-in-law." I pointed at Frank. "Sister-in-law." I twitched the finger over to Jan. "And wife." I flicked my thumb toward the other room.

"Then get in there with her. Don't come one more step into my crime scene. I'll question you in a minute."

I did as I was told and finally got Jen's attention as she looked up from her community cuddle. "Oh, BG, what are we going to do?" There were tears in her eyes and voice.

Often I was a wordsmith. After all, I wrote and talked for a living. It should be easy to come out with something pithy when pith is required. But confronted with a major portion of my life smashed beyond repair, the vision of Frank in a body-bag and Jan in jail and Jen and me with two more kids and way more Betty than I could take and Gary Semyenovic breathing down my neck and TBC one step away from a perp walk, all I could manage was, "Beats the hell out me."

Jen chose not to notice my profanity.

I wedged myself onto the couch next to Frank junior and took over consoling chores. That went on for what seemed like a long while but was probably no more than 10 minutes before Captain Pell and Detective Dellacourt came in.

"We're going to want to question the kids," Pell began.

"Not without me, you don't!" snapped Jen. I'd married a pit bull. "Don't you have people who specialize in kids?" The cop's sister-in-law had learned a thing or two.

"She's on the way. Maybe another half hour but who knows with this weather. Okay, how about we go over some basics?" Suddenly there was a pad and pen in his hands. He gestured to Jen. "Your name?"

"Jen Gaston. I'm Jan's twin."

"Not Jennifer?"

"Not Jannifer either."

"Hmmph," said Pell. "You look like sisters but not twins. You fraternal?"

"No, identical, but Jan broke her nose playing high school softball and they gave her a choice. Put it back the way it was or make it better. She chose a badge of honor."

Another "hmmph" from Pell, but he scribbled something in his pad. "Where were you earlier?"

Obviously, he meant, "when the murder occurred", but took it easy because of little ears.

"All day at the flower shop. About 7, I got my kids from my mom and went home until I got a call from Jan. I came over here as soon as Mom arrived to sit with the kids."

"How 'bout you?" he turned to me.

"I'm not a twin," I said. His look said "But you are an asshole" as I continued, "I was out doing road warrior duty with the storm for the last few hours. I've been on 422, 202, 10, the Blue Route, all over the western suburbs."

"Yeah," Dellacourt put in, "I heard you at 6, right after the accident. People got to be more careful."

I just nodded. "You know, every time I did a live shot, there's a record of which cell tower was used. You can check to make sure I wasn't "live on tape" so I could sneak over here and kill him."

Pell glared again. I couldn't tell if I'd just scuttled his pet theory or offended his sensibilities by suggesting I'd been involved.   "How'd you guys get along?"

I shrugged. "Not bad. We had a few laughs. I just saw him yesterday morning at the big warehouse fire scene. He scared the heck out of me, sneaking up in the dark. His idea of a joke."

"Did he seem okay?" That question surprised me.

"Yeah, sure.   He was joking around, busting on me as Jimmy Olsen. That was his pet name to annoy me."

"I'll keep that in mind," Pell deadpanned.

Just then the front door opened and a woman in a hooded winter coat with an ID dangling around her neck slipped in, shutting up behind her before many flakes could find it. She peeled back the hood and revealed one of the most stunning faces I'd ever seen.

She was about 35, with short dark hair that accented high cheekbones reddened more by Jack Frost than Maybelline. Blue searchlight eyes blazed left and right while slender fingers worked at the clasps of her coat. As she removed it, I turned away. There was only so much a married man could take.

"Captain Pell," she said, peeling a glove off and extending her hand, "Katrina Colarusso from Children's Services. I'm here to be what help I can be."

Pell shook her hand. "First thing, talk to the kids. Second, determine temporary custody."

"I want Mommy," Samantha whined right on cue although I don't think she actually knew what Pell was talking about.

"We'll take them!" Jen blurted. "They can come home with Aunt Jen and Uncle Bernie," and turning her attention toward Pell, "unless you have some objection."

Pell snorted. "None yet. Katrina, can you work in here? We have some.... stuff to do in the other room."

Pell and Dellacourt moved around the corner past Colarusso who finished stripping off her outerwear which she draped over a chair as delicately as possible. I tried to catch Jen's gaze to keep from looking at the other woman who moved past me leaving a hint of scent. The nose fixated on what the eyes avoided. She knelt down by Samantha and held the little girl's hands.

I took a cue and went back to the edge of the living room. Jan was still in her corner perch and the crime scene techs were putting away their camera gear. Pell and Dellacourt were looking at something near Frank's body. I squinted. It was a baseball bat, lying half under a chair a few inches from his outstretched right arm. Near Frank's other side, enclosed in an evidence bag, was a pistol, a 9mm, by the looks of it, probably Frank's service weapon. Past the body, a bit deeper in the house, his holster and ammo belt were curled up by a knee wall separating rooms.

I'm not a cop, but I can craft a theory out of thin air as well as the next guy and this air was getting mighty thick.

Let's see. We have a woman with a broken arm and a baseball bat on the floor near a dead cop whose service pistol is in an evidence bag nearby. Frank takes the bat to Jan? Jan takes the gun to Frank? Everybody's invited to the party.

Pell looked in my direction. "Hey, nosey, come with me." He motioned toward the kitchen so we walked around the evidence techs, their gear and the body past the empty holster through the dining room, and out to the back door in the kitchen. He flipped on the outside light which triggered one of those 300 watt halogens and brushed the darkness all the way back to the garage about 30 feet away. We both stared out the kitchen window. "What do you see?"

What jumped out in the winter vista was its only blemish, slowly being eroded by the storm, but there for now. "Footprints to the garage."

He nodded. "What's in the garage?"

Okay, so my normal smart-ass response would have been, "Duh, cars," but since he was being a mensch, I told him, "The usual junk. Some tools, sports gear, a couple of bikes, all wedged in around the cars."

"Maybe a baseball bat?"

Like the one in the living room, I thought. "Probably. Frank played some softball in the police league as his schedule allowed."

"Off-season. He might store it out there," Pell mused. "What size shoes does Frank wear?" Present tense. The body's not cold.

"Heck, I don't know. Doesn't Jan? Doesn't the Department? He'd have to buy uniform shoes. Why do you ask?"

Pell retreated into his own thoughts again. "Nothing, nothing."

I moved over to the back door. It was a slight change of perspective but I found myself looking right down the tracks to and from the garage, but that's not all there were. The central series seemed to be older, filling with new snow. There was another set to the side in which the footprints had sharper outlines and some were perpendicular to the line of travel.

Pell noticed me noticing. "The first thing the techs did was shoot those footprints with a fancy digital gizmo they have. They say they'll be able to make a pretty good model of the prints that way."

"What will that tell you?" I wanted to know.

"We'll see," Pell replied and flipped off the back light. Show's over.

Rather, this show was over. Just as we turned into the dining room, the front doors flew open and two figures. silhouetted by the glare of TV lights outside, entered. It was the Mayor and the Police Commissioner.

Any time a cop is shot or a firefighter hurt, let alone killed, it was must-see TV for the Mayor and the appropriate department head to be in front of the cameras. It not only showed their concern for the grieving family, but gave that take-charge impression that was so important in a public figure.

And it also got everyone else off the media hook for the moment. If you had the big fish, why bother with fry?

This, though, would be a sticky wicket.

The Mayor and Commissioner drew Captain Pell into a huddle. As he talked, they threw sullen glances Jan's way and she seemed to whither. The talk was brief and the Mayor and Commissioner left without extending condolences to the widow.

I knew the next act intimately and, in fact, I would have jumped in like another trained seal if I hadn't left my gear in the car. Looking out the front window, I saw the Mayor and Commissioner surrounded by cameras, high-beam lights and mike flags as soon as they hit the end of the walk. I don't know what they said but it lasted no more than 30 seconds before they ducked into the Mayor's SUV limo and were off in a cloud of slush. Reporters and photogs milled around for a moment on the sidewalk, sharing a collective "what the hell was that all about?" moment, then the reporters at least got in out of the storm.

There was a knock at the back door that Dellacourt raced to answer and two men from the Medical Examiner's office followed him into the living room.

"Go ahead," said one of the evidence techs and the first ME guy knelt and examined Frank with professional brevity. The second ME tech was unfolding a black bag which the two of them unceremoniously plunked Frank into and zipped closed. One grabbed a handle at the front and the other a handle at the back. They hoisted him knee high and maneuvered out through the dining room, kitchen and back door with no further ado.

It occurred to me that my colleagues outside were being screwed. The final shot they knew they needed was of the body bag, but the cops arranged for the ME van to pull into the back alley. The media either didn't know about the alley or had too few people on hand to send someone to stand there in the stormy dark for hours. It was the old back entrance trick.

Gotcha!

Now, Jan...

Pell went over and peered into the family room. When he pulled his head out, Katrina Colarusso followed and went over to my sister-in-law. They conversed in quiet tones for a moment and Colarusso nodded. Jan had begun to weep.

"No, no, not like this...." I heard her say and I guessed that the weight of what she had done was crushing. Detective Dellacourt cuffed her, albeit gently, and then helped her to her feet. Another officer draped her winter coat over her shoulders both for warmth and to obscure the cuffs and they headed for the front door.

Lights flared and voices shouted as they emerged but they hustled her into a police van that left immediately, followed for a short distance by photogs eager for that one last frame.

Captain Pell turned to me. "It looks as if you and your wife get to keep the kids. Children's Services will make the final determination but, for now, that's what Mrs. Tierney wants."

"Is she being charged?" I wanted to know.

"Not my call. This is way over my pay grade. It looks to me like she shot her husband to death. That's homicide unless it's in self-defense and with the bat there and the evidence of a physical altercation, we have to sort this out. I wouldn't be at all surprised if the Mayor, the Commissioner, the D.A. and the F.O.P. president all have lunch tomorrow."

The evidence technicians had left just after Jan. Pell, Dellacourt and the last remaining officer followed. Katrina Colarusso was putting on her coat.

"Here's my card," as she handed it to me. "Your wife already has one and I have your address and whatnot." As she talked, I found myself so drawn into her eyes that I had to struggle to follow her words. "We can fill out the appropriate papers later. Job one right now is to get those kids to a place of safety. Not here. Not with what they saw."

"What did they tell you?"

"Jen can fill you in." Katrina looked at me questioningly. "You know, I've seen you at other murder scenes, outside with them." She cocked her head toward the baying hounds just off the property line.

"I wish I was there now. It's easier."

"You might keep that in mind." she said, disapprovingly. "This city has, what, 300 murders a year. Every one has a moment like this, as a family confronts a vacuum that can never be filled. It hurts all over again to have it in the news. Sometimes it's too much coverage, sometimes too little, but it's never right."

I could have said something about the public's right to know, but that's crap because the public doesn't care who gets killed as long as it's not them or theirs.

I could have said something about how these were compelling stories and what we want to compel is people to watch, read or listen.

Or I could have said, it's just the nature of the beast, that none of the media troops outside really wanted to be here, now, except maybe Garrison Watts who would chase a cop-shooting down a street of broken glass barefoot. They'd like to be home with their families too, especially after a scene like this, but someone was paying each of them to stand in the snow or hide in the van to poke the story with a stick and see if anything came out.

This one hid a nest of hornets.

Chapter Ten

Katrina left and the photogs got obligatory shots of her even though they probably didn't know who the heck she was. Shame, though. She'd brighten up any TV screen.

I walked into the family room where Jen consoled Jan's kids. Frankie was collapsed on her lap, sound asleep. Samantha was fighting the good fight but Morpheus was about to win.

"What now?" she asked. "We can't stay here." And we couldn't escape just yet either.

I looked at my watch. "If we wait until 11:30 they should be gone." It was quarter of 11. Even with the storm, this was likely to be one of the top stories on the news. By 11:10 they'd be pulling down their microwave masts and reeling in cables and by 11:30 begin the long slippery process of returning to their various stations. The coast would then be clear.

Jen ruffled Samantha's hair gently. "My car is right in between two of those live trucks."

"Mine's down the street." No easy out. We sighed simultaneously. You live with someone and stuff like that happens.

Jen let Samantha's head touch down on the couch and repositioned little Frank so he was tucked in a corner formed by the arm and back. She slithered out from between them. "I'll go pack a bag. They'll need some clothes." So practical, my wife. I loved the heck out of her then.

That left me alone with Sam and Frankie so I did what any guy would do. I sat in a chair, turned on the TV and flicked through the stations with the remote. It was as mindless and meaningless as the programs I bypassed click by click looking for the Promised Land, the one thing that could take my mind off my troubles. Sadly, this cable outfit didn't carry the Vodka Channel.

Eleven o'clock arrived and I decided to see what Garrison Watts had to say outside the Tierney house about what had happened inside.

The show opened with the dual anchors quickly throwing to a split screen box effect, Garrison on one side with snow flying and meteorologist Nancy Johnson on the other, also in the snow. Thank God for weather people brave enough to go out in the weather. How would we know it was snowing otherwise?

They did a tease lead, where Nancy's scene expanded to full screen for a moment as she explained that it was snowing (no, really? If a picture is worth a thousand words, shut up!) and said she'd be back licketty-split to tell us how much it was snowing, where it was snowing and what flavor it was. After about 30 seconds of that, the Suicide Channel was looking pretty good.

Then her effects box retreated and Garrison's came forward. I mentally tuned back in.

"That's right, Nancy, tragedy in blue. Here in the City's Somerton section, a murder mystery tonight, with police officer Frank Tierney dead." Garrison's face was replaced by a still-shot of Frank, all spit-polished in his dress blues, the kind of photo that could be put in the glass-framed shrine of fallen officers in the Roundhouse, police headquarters. Garrison's voice continued on under the photo but it had changed pitch slightly, so I knew he had gone to tape. Most TV live-shots were only 10 percent live. The rest was a recorded piece in the middle that I've heard referred to as a Sony sandwich. Every newsroom has its own terms.

He talked about Frank, the blah-blah veteran, once decorated for blah-blah, and that the Mayor had come to call but offered up little.

Cut to sound on tape of the Mayor: "Officer Frank Tierney was killed this evening in circumstances that are yet unclear. His wife and two small children are unharmed, but that's all I'm going to say for now except that the investigation continues and our heart goes out to those who knew and loved Officer Tierney."

The camera cut back to Garrison live and there was a slight delay before he was cued. "Neighbors here tell me nothing but good things about Officer Tierney and his family. None had anything to add to the circumstances of his death. After all, as you can see, it's not a night to be outside. But for now, a police officer is dead and his killer, even what killed him, still unidentified. Garrison Watts, live in Somerton. Back to you, Kate and Doug."

The bobble head anchors returned and I left, at least mentally. This is one hot potato. Cops had domestic problems all the time. Jan and Jen's shop did a healthy business in make-up floral arrangements. A cop's wife leaves him, dime a dozen. A cop's wife kills him, that's a 1909 SVDB, a very rare coin indeed.

Jen came back about the time they finally got around to the weather. Six to 8 inches, get ready to shovel in the morning. Tune in for school closings.

I peeked out front. Only one live truck remained and I could see by its interior light that the photographer was stowing the last of his gear.

"We can make a move shortly," I told Jen. "We better get the kids in their snowsuits." Now, that was a challenge. Even when awake, it was a chore to dress children for winter, slipping each limb into its proper sleeve, battening down the hatches until they looked like little

Michelin men with idiot mittens. Samantha stirred enough to be some help. Frankie was as limp as a doll and we had to pull his arms and legs through the snowsuit.

Finally, when they were dressed, I scouted the situation by taking the suitcases (yes, Jen had packed two) out to her car. I touched the key remote and the trunk popped open. It could be a tight fit. Not only was the usual junk in there, but a computer, including the processor box, flat screen monitor, printer, scanner and a jumble of wires. I moved things around and placed the suitcases in. There, plenty of room.

Back inside, I hoisted Samantha over my shoulder. Jen held Frankie in burp position, a set of keys in her free hand. Leaving, she locked the front door but as she turned away from it she slipped on the icy stoop. Her right foot hit the next step hard and she twisted off to the side, dropping into a row of bushes with a thud and a puff of snow.

I rushed to her side as best I could, without dropping my bigger burden. "Jen, are you all right? Jen!"

Frankie began to cry, startled awake. Jen looked at me dully. If life were a cartoon, various symbols would be rotating through her eyes until they settled on "tilt". "Oooooh," was about all she could manage.

"Let me put Sam in the car and I'll call 911."

"No, no," she said, struggling to rise. I planted my feet and, against my better judgment, gave her a hand up. She immediately went down on one knee with a gasp of pain.

"We have to take you to the ER."

"It's nothing. I'll be all right." With my help, she hobbled down the worn footprints in the snow. I buckled Sam in the back seat of Jen's car, then relieved her of Frankie to do the same. She plopped into the driver's seat, her face pale when it should have been winter blushed.

"Jen..." I said, knowing we should be planning our route to the nearest hospital.

"I'll be all right," she said in a hushed tone, and swung her legs into the car. I considered protesting more but figured, wait and see. This drive home will show her. We'll hand Sam and Frankie off to Betty and take her to the ER.

After I recovered my car, we made slow progress through the snow, which was coming down hard. There would be, as promised, six to eight inches on lawns, maybe a little less on streets due to some initial melting but that created the risk of underlying ice. You could approach a stop sign at 10 miles an hour, hit the brakes and sail right on through.

Fortunately, there was almost no traffic and we made the 10-minute dual drive home in about half an hour.

I took charge of both kids, then the luggage, while Jen struggled to muscle herself vertical. It was all she could do to stand there, gripping the top of the car door and the roof, until I returned to her side child-free.

"One last chance," I offered. "Just get back in the car. Betty will tuck Sam and Frankie in and we'll go over to Aria-Torresdale. " The nearest ER.

She looked at me then kindly even lovingly, taking one gloved hand off the car to touch my face gently. "Not tonight, hon. We'll see in the morning."

I helped her hobble into the house where she collapsed on a couch in the living room, intertwined with her niece and nephew. They were once again sound asleep. One of the only bits of good advice we'd ever gotten about parenting was, never wake a sleeping baby. If there's something wrong, they'll let you know.

So I concentrated on getting Jen out of her coat and boots. She sucked air through gritted teeth when I removed the right one. "Get me some ice," she suggested.

I hung up her coat and put the boots in the gunk tray by the door. In the kitchen, I grabbed a Ziploc bag and poured about a dozen ice cubes into it, before resealing it, wrapping it in a dishtowel and returning to Jen.

She clamped it on her right ankle and managed a brave smile. "Thanks, hon. I don't know what I'd do without you."

"All part of the service." Warmed by her complement, I leaned in and kissed her forehead. "I better take care of the kids, and your mother."

I found Betty asleep in the family room, the TV whispering as background noise. I hadn't noticed her, or she me, as I tromped through to the kitchen for ice. I stared at her for a moment. Yeah, she was a pain in the tush sometimes but, in a crisis, she was the go-to gal. Both my parents were dead so mother-in-law was as close as I got to a "mother" any more.

I did some quick calculations. I could wedge Sam and Frankie here and there in the house, at least for one night, without disturbing Betty. It would be unkind, at the very least, to kick her out given the weather right then, so why wake her at all?

I went upstairs and, after a peek at Elizabeth sleeping angelically, went into Lorraine's room. She too was in the lap of the gods, radiant with the innocence of young slumber. I needed some of that then. I'd need more, later.

But from her closet I pulled an inflatable mattress. It was queen-size and the only place I could fit it on the second floor was our room. So much for any intimacy tonight but that had pretty much gone out the window with Jen's slip and fall.

The mattress had a built-in pump so 30 seconds after plugging it in it was plump enough. I twisted closed the stopper and went to fetch some sheets and blankets.

That took me a few minutes so by the time I get back to Jen, she had moved the icepack to her head and was lying back like some diva in a swoon. I left her alone as I stripped, redressed and went to tuck-in Samantha and Frankie. I pushed the mattress up against a wall so Frankie couldn't fall off, gave each of them a stuffed animal and a kiss.

Jesus, what a night, I thought. The world they knew was gone, literally blown away. What on earth are they supposed to make of this, that Mommy killed Daddy? Can you say "counseling, for life?"

Jen had the ice back on her ankle when I returned to her side. Questions bubbled inside me but Jen hated it when I squeezed answers out of her like I would an interview subject. She beat me to the punch.

"They'd been having trouble, bad. Jan had even called the domestic abuse line over the weekend, left a message, but never acted on it. They'd tell her to leave. She couldn't. I know, I know, that's like the abused wife's refrain. I can 't leave him. He wuvs me." There was scorn in her tone.

"I was here with the kids when she called all freaked out. 'Jen, Jen, I shot him', she said. They had argued. It got physical. He left the room and she thought he'd gone to cool down, but he came back in with that baseball bat, and swung it, smacked her in the arm. She grabbed his gun and shot him, killed him. Oh, my God, even in self-defense, this is horrible,"

"Yes, but we'll get through this. We're family, you, me, Jan and Betty."

"Thanks, B.G, thanks." I could tell she wanted to put this, and herself, to bed. For the moment, I let it go.

"You want some help, upstairs?"

"No, just get me a blanket and I'll spend the night here. It'll be better in the morning, you wait and see."

The morning....

I couldn't go to work, not with this kind of turmoil. I had to let them know, so after getting Jen settled I went upstairs to our room, took the cordless phone into the bathroom and called the newsroom. No one was in overnight when we let the network go on uninterrupted so I left a message.

"Hi, this is Bernie. I can't come in today. The police officer who was shot to death last night in his home, Frank Tierney, was my brother-in-law. His wife, my wife's sister, was arrested and we have to see how this sorts itself out. It looks like a domestic, baseball bat versus gun, but we'll have to wait and see. Look, I'll call you in the morning. Put this down as a personal day or something. Mental health day. God, I hope I get some."

Take Two, A Smart-ass Mystery

I hung up the phone. I managed to brush my teeth and change into pajamas before I passed out almost on contact with the sheets.

Chapter Eleven:
Wednesday

I awakened to the phone beedooping or whatever the heck you call the noise it made and I rolled out of bed to grab it before Sam and Frankie stirred. "Hello," I croaked, but not much came out. I looked through the window. It was sort of light outside, tough to tell with snow and cloud cover.

"You fucking asshole, what's wrong with you?" began the man on the other end. It went downhill from there, profanity-wise.

"Hey, hey, hey," tried to interject, softly, so as not to wake Sam and Frankie, but it wasn't working. Finally, I just hung up.

The phone rang again in a moment. I answered with, "Are you ready to play nice?"

"This is Captain Pell and I should have you arrested twice now! Twice! Once for last night. I never should have let you in! You fucking reporters just can't turn it off, just can't let us do our jobs without sticking your nose in it."

"Whoa, whoa, Captain. I've got sleeping kids in the room with me, Frank's kids. Can you just tone it down a notch and tell me why you're so pissed off?"

"Don't play me for a fool, Gaston, at least don't do it twice. I gave you access last night, let you see just what we saw, just what we have to deal with, and you blab it all over the radio."

"What? Captain, I came home and went to bed. I didn't file anything on this, nothing! I didn't even tell anyone..." My voice trailed off as a horrible thought occurred to me. I looked at the clock: 7:28. "Listen, give me your number."

"I'm not giving you my number, fuck-head! Call public affairs and let them ignore you."

"All right, you have my number. Call me back in ten minutes."

"Why? What do you think....."

I hung up on him. Time was of the essence. I tiptoed around the bodies on the inflated mattress. Sam still looked like an angel, but Frankie was propped up against the wall as if he'd gotten stuck doing a headstand and just stayed put. The phone rang once more even before I took my third step.

In the shower stall, I turned on the radio and rotated the tuner to WPN just in time to hear the network outcue.

There was a short local jingle then "We're Philly's News. This is Anthony Freeman."

"And I'm Tina Lowell. In the news this morning, blood and snow."

"We'll check in with Weather Central in a moment. All Philadelphia public and Archdiocesan schools closed today, but our top story is a murder in our own extended family."

Oh, fuck, I thought, tapping my forehead on the shower tile.

Tina picked up the story. "A 38 year old City policeman was killed in his Somerton home. More from We're Philly's News reporter Bernie Gaston."

My own voice came out of the speaker. It was phone quality (which is to say, lousy) and I sounded as almost as dead as a Middle East hostage in one of those "Allah is great" videos, but it was what I had feared. They had taken my voicemail message and massaged it with digital snips here and there. They had even taken one of my lockouts from another report, filtered it to sound like phone quality and tacked it on the end. So here's what I heard myself say:

"Police officer Frank Tierney was shot to death in his home last night. His wife was arrested. It looks like a domestic, baseball bat versus gun, but we'll have to see. Bernie Gaston, WPN News."

My head hit the wall again, a little harder.

No wonder Pell was pissed. Some of what I'd said in the phone message was more than what Garrison Watts had had in his live shot at 11, more than what the Mayor had let on.

I went back into the bedroom where the phone had stopped ringing but I heard Betty downstairs calling, "Bernie, there's a man on the phone for you, a Captain Pell."

I picked up the extension softly. "I know what happened!" I jumped in, hoping to cut him off in mid-cuss.

"Nice lady, your mother-in-law," Pell said. He seemed to have left the land of homicidal emotion for tar-and-feather-ville. "So what happened, and this better be good."

I told him about the voicemail and admitted that I probably said too much but not nearly as much as I could have said if I really had wanted to tell all. I also admitted that I, too, was jagged off about this. They had no right.

"Welcome to my world," said Pell. "I deal with you people all the time."

"Listen," I said, maybe trying to change the subject or, for some reason, get back in his good graces, "you guys know about the real estate trust that owns that arson job the other night?"

"It's not my case, but I'll pass it along. What do you know?"

I told him what Agent Semyenovic had shown me about the Rosen-Philadelphia Real Estate Investment Trust and its apparent over-insuring of the building.

"Thanks. I'll see if the Arson Squad knows this. But I want to make something clear, real crystal clear. You can be family or you can be a reporter but not both. Don't you ever fuck with my case again."

I wanted to say I hadn't fucked with it at all but this didn't seem like the time for semantics so I agreed.

As soon as he hung up, I dialed the station.

"WPN, Silcox."

"This is Bernie. Where do you guys get off putting my private voicemail message on the air?"

"It's not private. It belongs to us and so do you. That's not my opinion. That's TBC's, exactly. You know, you could have avoided this entire thing if you had actually filed something. Then we would not have had to, out of desperation, use your groundbreaking, insider information. Your scoop. Did I say "scoop?" That's so Front Page. Stop the presses! Oh, and TBC says you can come in about noon."

"Noon? I need the day! Do you have any idea how...."

"Don't cry on my shoulder, Beanie. I might put your tears on the radio. Noon. Be here or be square. See you." He hung up.

Samantha was stirring but Headstand Boy was still having upside down dreams. I shut the door to the bedroom behind me and tiptoed downstairs. There was no point my stealth since everyone else was up, most gathered around the kitchen table.

Jen was still wearing last night's clothes, which as much as anything told me she was hurting. There was an Advil bottle sitting near her teacup and I expect she'd taken a maximum dose. Her hair was a mess from sleeping on the couch and she hadn't yet brushed it out.

"How are you feeling?" I asked as I gave her a peck on the cheek. Ask me no questions and I'll tell you no lies, is a phrase that popped into my head.

"It hurts but I'll be okay. I made it all the way in here, didn't I?" Whoa, thirty feet. Alert the Philadelphia Marathon.

"Made it by hanging on the furniture like a sloppy drunk," said Betty.

"Sloppy drunk," said Lorraine, a few chunks of kid-kibble falling back into her cereal bowl as she spoke.

"I'm tired," Elizabeth yawned from the couch where she sat with a Pop Tart and the TV remote.

"You shouldn't be," Grandma told her. "You slept like a log last night. Honestly, Jen, you put the girls to bed so early, I thought sure they'd be fussing or waking up at 3 a.m."

"I know my girls, mom," said Jen. "I thought they were coming down with something, so Dr. Gaston prescribed Nyquil and bed rest."

"No wonder they slept," said Betty. "But I don't think you're supposed to give Nyquil to kids."

Lorraine hopped down from her chair and began excavating the toy box in the family room as I grabbed a Diet Coke. Now, there's a benefit from having my mother-in-law in the house. Someone must have restocked the fridge.

I sat next to Jen nursing her steaming cup. I didn't break the companionable silence for a moment until I remembered my bad news. "I have to go in today. I asked for the day off but Nash says I have to come in at noon."

"That's a shame, hon." Jen patted my hand. "But we can manage. School's canceled in Benfranklin. Although I don't know about the shop. Maybe I can call Melissa (her part-timer) to open up today."

"What's with the computer in your trunk?" I asked, only because it had just occurred to me. She blew across the cup and then took a long drink.

"It was Jan's. It's broken. She gave it to me yesterday, before, before all this. She brought it into the shop and said, here, take this piece of crap."

I didn't know what to make of that. Jen hadn't mentioned the computer yesterday, but I supposed that was understandable given that a lot had been going on.

"Do we need a computer?" I asked, and my thinking was "no". I had my laptop and could connect wirelessly from anywhere in the house. That thing in the trunk was circa so two years ago, which meant obsolete.

"So then we'll throw it out." She tried to make it sound reasonable but it frankly sounded bitchy. "I thought the kids could use one."

This was not our plan. Our plan had been to hold off on computer use for the girls. Sure, they teach valuable skills, but also teach sitting on your butt i-m-ing drooling perverts.

TV is one thing, plotzed down mindlessly in front of the electronic hearth but the internet, now essentially factory installed in all computers, is a dark alley where the mindless, morals-less and inhibition-less await you.

But I let the issue drop while I ate an English muffin and then suited up to do battle with the snow. The good news about our townhouse complex was that the township plowed the streets. The bad news was they usually did it just as you got done shoveling out the car. One instant: good to go. The next: there's a three-foot snow dam blocking you in and the plow driver heading off, waving cheerily.

So I started on the walk, which wasn't all that long, even though we had an end unit. I was brushing the snow from the cars, including Betty's, when a thought came to me. I popped Jen's trunk, and transferred the computer into mine. Let's see what my "little guy", my cyber repair guru, would say.

It was 9:30 or so when the plow arrived and blocked me in. As I launched into round two of shoveling, Betty had the kids in their snowsuits running around the back and side yards like maniacs. With her guidance, they tried to build a snowman but the snow was so light it would hardly stick together. They had a great time throwing clouds of flakes at each other.

I managed to catch a shower before leaving. I checked in with the newsroom and they told me there was a 1:00 with the Managing Director on the snow emergency.

That would be downtown and gave me plenty of time to take care of the computer.

My "little guy" was in a strip of shops along Frankford Avenue near the bug museum. He wasn't open when I got there but he lived right upstairs and responded to my ringing the bell by answering the door and ushering me in.

I don't even know if his shop had a name. All it said on the sign outside was "Computers" but Comp-u-pit would have been appropriate or Digital Dump or Silicon Slob. You get the idea.

Oliver Osteen was "The 40 year old Virgin" meets "The Nutty Professor," a social pariah with a genius IQ who told me the last time I'd been there that, rather than go to the dentist, he'd pulled two of his own teeth with a pair of pliers normally used for removing motherboards. He could have been a "cue the creepy music" sort of guy, lurking around the middle school offering kids free fiber optics. But Ollie was a sweetheart, albeit a demented sweetheart. If he'd jumped out of a dark corner, not even Chicken Little would run off.

"I have a computer I want you to look at."

"What's wrong with it?"

"I have no idea. My wife got it from her sister who says it's broken."

"A mystery. My favorite kind."

I brought the box into his store since he was still in slippers and placed it on a glass counter through which I could see a chip morgue. What the Mütter Museum in Center City does for preserved body parts displayed in bottles of formaldehyde, Ollie's store did for silicon parts. There was a tower of monitors in one corner, some teetering, others cracked. Processor boxes were stacked like insulation along the walls. On the counter was a Mac laptop, its screensaver alive with Monty Python characters bouncing around.

He scribbled out a receipt and told me he'd call. I chatted with him a few minutes because it seemed like the right thing to do. He didn't even take a deposit. He knew I was good for it.

I had some time before the Managing Director's newser so I meandered up and down streets in the Northeast to see if they'd been plowed. The majors were okay, slush-covered and sometimes reduced a lane due to brown snow piled against parked cars, but okay given the light traffic. The back streets were often snow-covered as the City, always looking to save a buck, seemed to depend on the snow removal technique known as spring.

I got some interviews with retired people out clearing the walk who were only too happy to bitch about the Mayor. They didn't have any place to go anyway but it was the principle of the thing. I recorded the scrape-scrape of their shovels and the roar of a nearby snow blower. Then a city plow truck came by and not only completely blocked their little street but left my car looking like a chocolate chip sundae.

We laughed because tears might have frozen and began shoveling and snow blowing again.

I got to the Managing Director's office about 12:45. The dayside media hordes were there, many having been on the clock since 3:00 a.m. so it was not a lively bunch. Everybody else talked, sharing subdued complaints and war stories. I kept quiet. Anything I might say could and would be used against me, it seemed.

The thing began 15 minutes late, which was spot-on according to Lianne-time. Lianne Rodriguez, Philadelphia's Managing Director, had the juggling skills of an air traffic controller, the personality of the Borg on Star Trek and absolutely no regard for journalists' deadlines.

She blathered through a prepared five minute statement which said, paraphrasing now, we did great. The long version was, we did great but PennDOT can kiss my sweet Puerto Rican ass.

Oh, well. We could only quote the spokesperson we're given.

As I left City Hall, I ran into Captain Pell. More accurately, he and another man were waiting for me. He introduced Lt. Church of the Arson Squad who picked up the conversation.

"Captain Pell passed your tip along to me, but frankly I'm mystified. Where did you say you got this?"

"From the FBI. I was with Agent Gary Semyenovic yesterday morning on, well, another matter, and he told me, showed me documents that looked official enough to me."

"Hmm," said Church, turning to Pell. "I've called this Semyenovic, left two messages and haven't heard back."

"I'll reach out to the Special Agent-in-Charge. He's a decent sort for a Fed. We'll rattle the tree." He slapped me on the shoulder. "Loose lips sink ships. Later." Pell and Church walked off toward the Criminal Justice Center.

Rattle the tree, my ass, I thought. Rattle me. This was getting way too deep, being involved in two criminal investigations at once. Reporting on two at once would have been enough for one day.

I went back to the car, wrote the story with the Managing Director's placid account of storm response combined with the griping from the Northeast and uploaded the text and audio. I hoped to avoid going into the office, but my phone rang and I was summoned to a meeting with the boss.

I drove out the Schuylkill dreading the worst but not really knowing what that might be. I'd been seeing so much downside lately that a dirt nap was looking like an hour in a hammock on a warm summer day.

I hardly ever saw Bill Henry, the News and Programming Director at WPN. The truth is, he was a pal of Hank O'Hare's from before Noah learned what a cubit was, and that was probably the only reason O'Hare could hold down a job. Henry, a long-winded teller of tales from when he was at a network, put in about a two hour day, 10 to noon. Then it was lunchtime and that meant a liquid lunch and the rest of the day he was simply unavailable. When I first arrived at the station about five years earlier, it fried my bacon that he was a lush, a letch and a loser, but perhaps I had matured in that I soon dropped "loser" from my assessment. Even when drunk, he was a shrewd judge of talent and manipulator of people, who managed to keep TBC at bay on one side, and herd a staff of cats on the other.

This day, though, Henry was sober as I got into his office about mid-afternoon. It didn't auger well, I knew, that he had "skipped a meal", probably on my account.

"Sit down," he offered/ordered when I got into his office. It was nothing much to look at but, like Nash's, in a place where most of us had only a shared desk or common cubicle, it conveyed a certain status. He waited a moment after I sat, allowing my agitation to build. "We have to talk about your.....situation."

I didn't reply, or even ask, "Which situation?" There were so many.

When he sensed I wouldn't volunteer anything, he resumed, "This cop-murder story. Look, I'm sorry. I know he was your brother-in-law and your sister-in-law is the suspect. But this is great stuff! Gina is out right now at a newser by a women's group, rallying on Jan Tierney's behalf as an abused wife. We can really gain some ground here, Bernie. This is a story people want to know about and you are on the inside."

"Bill, so far today, I've been shouted at, insulted and threatened on the phone by the lead homicide detective in this case, and then approached by him and another cop as I was on the snow story in Center City. Somehow they knew right where I would be. Even if it would be ethical for me to have anything to do with covering this, I can't. Captain Pell has already made it clear he'll arrest me."

"He can't do that," Henry replied as if saying it made it so.

"This is nonsense, you know. It shouldn't even be getting this far. You want to cover this story? Have Gina call Captain Pell or go up to Somerton and nose around the neighborhood. This'd be a good day for it. People would be out shoveling."

"They're all on the outside of the story. You're the one who was there."

"Thanks for reminding me, and no thanks, by the way, for that little trick with the voicemail this morning. That's why I'm on the cops' shit list.

"Why'd she do it, Bernie? Why'd your sister-in-law shoot her husband? Is she a victim or villain? That's the story we need to be telling!"

"Then someone other than me needs to tell it! I have her kids living at my house, for Pete's sake! I've had Thanksgiving dinner at their house, walked right over the spot where his body was last night. There is so little objectivity in me about this, my head is spinning."

"You did all right on the voicemail."

"No, you did all right or Silcox or whoever re-arranged my message. I was in no condition to tell a coherent story."

Henry steepled his hands over his mouth and nose and sighed. This couldn't have been news to him, I thought.

"Let me be frank," he said finally. "TBC, Mr. Nash, insists."

"What about impartiality?"

Henry shrugged. "He doesn't care."

"Conflict of interest?"

"Doesn't care."

"My ass getting busted?"

"We'll send you a cake with a file inside. Bernie, this is all bullshit. The cops aren't going to arrest you. This is a First Amendment issue. They can't muzzle you."

"But they don't have to talk to me, either. Captain Pell was very open with me last night."

"So you do know more than you're letting on."

"Never said I didn't but the moment I put it on the air is the last time that will be true. After that, 9-1-1 won't take my calls. Pell made that plain."

"Pell doesn't sign your paychecks."

That comment hung in the air like the mother of all farts. I swear to God, if he couldn't tell how much this stunk, he needed a nose transplant.

My mind flashed over options (few) and consequences (bad). More to buy time than anything else, I said, "Give me a couple of minutes, Bill. I need to call home."

He nodded and I headed to the newsroom. Cell phone coverage in the swamp was iffy.

Betty answered. "We wondered where you'd been. Jen's pretty upset."

"No doubt," I replied, what with all that's happening. "Put her on. How's your foot?" I asked as soon as I heard the phone change hands.

"Where's that computer?" she barked, oblivious to the question. "What did you do with it? Why did you go into my car?"

"I took it to get fixed." Here was another reason to be sitting down when I called home, the hairpin turns. "You said it was broken. You certainly weren't going to get around to it, so I took it to Oliver for the once-over."

"I said it was broken, not that it needed to be fixed." Jen's voice was cold. "I was just going to throw it out."

This made no sense to me, inasmuch as she had suggested we keep it and that kind of presupposed fixing it. We didn't need a doorstop that big, but I had enough sense remaining not to say so. I did what any red-blooded American husband would do. I groveled.

"Aw, hon, it'll be all right. If it costs too much to repair, I'll tell Oliver to keep it. That's as good as throwing it out. And if he does fix it, we can hide it away. Maybe Betty wants it. It won't upset our arrangement with computers and the kids."

"You have to get it back." So much for groveling.

"Listen, this is nuts! I called to see how you were holding up. How's your foot? How are the kids, ours and theirs? Have you heard from Jan? How are you emotionally? I also have something coming down on my head like a load of bricks. You know what they want me to do? Report on this case! I'm supposed to be their inside guy, their ticket to bigger ratings."

I was trying to keep my voice down but I'm not very good at that. Others in the newsroom were looking at me. I swear some were taking notes. Finally, I hissed, "I'm half tempted to tell them to take this job and shove it."

There was a moment of silence before Jen said in a small voice, "That wouldn't be a good idea. Melissa says we've only had one customer today at the shop. No cops. Zero. Word gets around." Cops don't go to a cop killer for flowers.

There was a moment where neither of us spoke, mutely considering the unfolding mess.

"Well," I asked finally, "how are you holding up?"

"I still can't get around much. Mom's all over me to call the doctor. I probably should at this point." Sure, I thought bitterly, you ignore me and listen to Betty when we're saying the same thing. "Elizabeth and Lorraine are fine. They think having their cousins over is one big game. Samantha and Frankie have been quiet, except when they ask about their mom. I got a call from some lawyer who says Jan asked her to represent her."

"What lawyer?" I had a bad feeling about this, it being a domestic abuse case.

"I don't know. I'm not with it today. Holiday? Hoolihan?"

Oh, no. "Hanratty?" I volunteered. "Lisette Hanratty?"

"That's it. You know her?"

"I've seen her in court a few times. She's beyond a pit bull. She's a wolverine with an Uzi. She specializes in domestic abuse cases and I have seen her rip any witness who doesn't buy her argument that the woman is always right, to shreds."

"I talked with her for a moment. She seemed very committed."

"She ought to be committed," I responded although I meant to a mental institution. Hanratty was to law what a roadside bomb was to a birthday party.

"She said she'd been hired by the Delaware Valley Domestic Violence Action League." The DVDVAL was an in-your-face activist group that seemed to recommend lynching for pinching a woman's bottom. Don't get me wrong, I reject pinching, stroking, groping or whatever. I have never hit Jen, never even considered it, but DVDVAL gals were, frankly, brownshirts. More than one man accused of abuse had suffered mysterious "falls" which looked suspiciously like a curb-stomp by some pointy-toed boots. And that was before the trial.

"Has Jan been charged?"

"Not yet. The lawyer called about an hour ago."

"They're going to have to get to it. The clock started ticking last night about 10:30. They have 24 hours to charge or release."

"She said she'd call back."

I was working a few angles in my head. This new information might get me off the hook at work. Things were happening in a hurry.

"Listen, hon," I said. "You hang in there. I don't know how late they're going to make me work but I'll let you know. I'll call later to see if you need me to pick anything up on the way home."

"How about that computer," she suggested.

"Go get your foot looked at and you'll be well enough to get it yourself. See you later.

I put the phone down and turned to Carrie Swoboda. "I have to get back in with Bill, but have someone call Lisette Hanratty, the attorney. Ask her about Jan Tierney, her new client. When I get out, I'll call the cops and the D.A. They're going to have to charge Jan or let her go shortly."

I had been gone, what, 10 minutes but when I knocked on Bill Henry's door, I heard a momentary scramble inside and the clink of ice on glass. He summoned me in and I found him sitting much as I had left him but with a guilty expression. I smelled alcohol in the air and was tempted to ask for some.

"Listen, Bill," I went on instead, "I was thinking about what you said and we can find some middle ground. What if I find out what I can and feed the newsroom what I can?

Point us in the right direction? Look, I already told Carrie that Lisette Hanratty has been hired to represent Jan." Henry gave me a blank look. "She's the domestic violence battleaxe, defended Mary Metzger in the Lovers Lane murder. Metzger went necking with her boyfriend, got him drunk and naked and while he was indisposed dropped the car into a reservoir, him inside it. She argued battered woman's syndrome and Hanratty sold it to the jury."

"She's one stone cold bitch," said Henry.

"Also, I'm going to press the cops and D.A. They have to make a move soon. The only question is whether they want to make a big splash, in which case they'll charge Jan by 5 p.m., or not, in which case they'll slip her into arraignment court real quiet. Of course, with Hanratty around, nothing is quiet."

"Good, good," Henry said, nodding. One nod looked like his head hit his chest and stayed there. Then he startled. "Keep up the good work." He gestured me out. The audience was over, for now.

Behind me as I left, I heard that clinking again.

Chapter Twelve

Carrie had a phone wedged between her head and shoulder when I got back into the newsroom. "Listen," I heard her say, "can we do some tape? Can I record you?" Pennsylvania is strict about making sure interview subjects know they are being recorded, so we don't even touch the "record" button until they agree. This was evidently a tough fight. "No, no, Lisette, we are going to be there afterward. We'll go to the D.A's thing and then yours outside, but I just need a moment with you now. You've already told me what's going on. Just tell me on tape." We hadn't actually used tape in years but the terminology stuck. It was better than saying, "Just give it to me digitally." That sounded like a come-on to a proctologist.

Carrie apparently didn't get anywhere and signed off frustrated. She turned to me. "Bernie, this is going to be one major circle jerk. The D.A. is doing his thing at 4:30. Lisette Hanratty says Jan Tierney is being charged with homicide and they will ask for no bail."

I just nodded. I had expected as much, the general charge of homicide, for causing the death of another person, which Jan admitted to Jen she'd done. I didn't know what she'd told the cops.

"You want me to go to this?" Actually, despite my pissing and moaning about conflict of interest, I wanted to be there.

"Yeah, and Hanratty promises a demonstration outside the D.A.'s office."

"A three-ring circus. All we're missing is the bearded lady."

"Huh," Carrie grinned, "I thought that's all they had in the DVDVAL." We both laughed. "Gina already filed on their newser, so there may not be much new when Hanratty finally speaks but Gina will cover her and you go cover the D.A."

"What did they have to say?"

"They're shocked, shocked, that a brutalized wife is being charged. They say your sister-in-law called the domestic abuse hotline over the weekend. You know anything about that?"

"Nope." I lied flawlessly. While Jen had mentioned the call, I didn't know what it said so I'd look like an even bigger idiot that I hadn't asked. Frank certainly hadn't said anything although the last time I'd seen him he hadn't been all that talkative, what with the two bullets in his chest and all.

I changed the subject. "I'll probably do a couple of live shots tonight and then a report or two, but what about morning?" A.M. drive, the morning rush hour to everyone else, is radio's bread and butter, even though at a station like WPN it was more like bread and water.

"Sounds good. Oh," she turned and grabbed a piece of paper from the landfill of her desk, "this guy called for you again. Something about MLK Day of Service."

I looked at the note. Marc Solarz, putting the "load" in "PR load". I checked the clock and reluctantly decided I had enough time to call him, but all I got was his voicemail, as usual, and I sure wasn't going to risk another tongue-lashing by Conan the receptionist just to give them some publicity.

I drove back to Center City under the sharp western edge of the weather system that had kicked us around overnight. The eastern sky was a sheet of slate-grey clouds being chased out by a clear late-day blue. It was going to be a cold night.

The D.A.'s office was on what amounted to the traffic square around City Hall. I had to ease my car into a small space in the Parkway press zone and play snow-mound hopscotch to get there. Bundled up pedestrians looked down as they walked, scanning for ice, slush or even the unexpected puddle. By the time I gotten a couple of blocks, I'd stepped in ankle-deep water (saved by my boots!) and windmilled my arms twice to prevent falling.

I trouped through the Hall's ground level arched walkways (and now wind tunnels) and the central courtyard where a hunched municipal worker still battled the fallen snow with a two-wheeled motorized plow and maybe it was its racket that prevented me from noticing the cacophony beyond.

There was no missing it once I got into the southern walkway. Northbound Broad Street traffic was at a standstill. There were two police cars canted up on the sidewalk, lights and flashers dazzling in the dim canyons between big buildings, as they tried to reduce three lanes of traffic to two or one. It was a tight fit. Once I turned the corner and could see the D.A.'s office, the problem became clear.

A couple dozen, maybe as many as fifty people, many waving protest signs, marched in a long oval, going one way on the sidewalk, the other in the street. They were chanting, horns were honking and I could hear a bullhorn, with all that sound bounding around among the stone-clad towers.

I stepped out into the gridlock, never mind the crosswalk, and did a nifty broken-field jog across to the demonstration. It was the DVDVAL gals, all right. They waved hastily-made signs, one reading "No tyranny for Tierney", and another "0 tolerance for domestic abuse." The zero actually looked like a gun sight's crosshairs.

TV crews swarmed and I could see a couple of live trucks half or full up on nearby curbs. This was a tough place to get a microwave signal out of at the best of times. This was not the best of times.

I spotted Gina Ginelli over near the bullhorn babe, but trying to stay out of the line of ire. The bullhorn was putting out jackhammer decibels and our medical plan didn't cover busted eardrums.

"What a party!" I shouted as I got close.

"These people are as rabid as Cujo," Gina yelled back. "They actually think she should be let go."

"Street theater," I pronounced, "and all for little old us. Carrie says, you cover Lisette Hanratty's post-newser newser. I'll cover the D.A."

"So you get to go inside to get warm and leave a damsel out here freezing her buns off?"

"That's about the size of it." I patted her on the shoulder chummily and headed toward the D.A.'s office entrance.

"I should sic these harpies on you," she called after me. I thought Gina was all right.

As I neared the public entrance, I saw Garrison Watts cozied up with Lisette Hanratty, not in a sexual way, but conspiratorial. They were talking, lip to ear, each phrase a poof of steam. I couldn't hear a word of it, but as I passed them, Garrison gestured to his photog who handed his tripod and some miscellaneous gear bag to the lawyer, she swept her coat collar up high and they all marched into the foyer with me.

Oh, this should be interesting, I thought, as I approached the receptionist who was behind bulletproof glass. I picked up a wall phone.

"Yes?"

"Hi, I'm Bernie Gaston from WPN, here for the D.A.'s newser."

The functionary, a barely-shaven man wearing an Islamic skullcap, looked up from his Koran. His eyes flicked from person to person, camera to tripod and Garrison's TV-familiar face, and a door buzzed off to the left. The photog nudged it with his snow-soaked boot and we were in. Lisette too, although her disguise wouldn't have fooled anyone who really looked. I'm sure they used her picture for darts practice in some parts of the building.

We rode an escalator up to a mezzanine area and marched into a media room where the podium already had a mike and the mult-box was built in to the wall. The sound would have hiss, but it'd be a high-class hiss.

I set up on a nearby table and attempted not to spend all of my time watching Lisette try to hide in plain sight. She'd brought an Inquirer and made a great show of reading yesterday's news as the curtain was about to rise on today's.

The other TV and radio stations' people straggled in and soon the floor of the media room was a forest of tripod legs. The mult-box sprouted a few cables like mine but also wireless mike transmitters that gave off a red-eyed, power-on glare.

Suddenly, someone slid into a seat beside me. It was Sarah Tilson, who had peeled off her winter coat revealing a clingy cashmere sweater and tight black pants, which I wouldn't have minded if she'd peeled off as well. She smelled like honey.

"Hi, Bernie, let me cut to the chase." You have to like a woman who knows what she wants. "We need some kind of comment from Jan Tierney's family. The Tierneys themselves aren't talking or, with the one or two who did say something, I can't put it on TV. How about, after this little circle jerk, and Lisette gets done," she cocked her head at the woman behind the paper, "How fucking funny is that? How about you say a little something for the family? "

"I don't know." I really didn't. I could end up quoting myself. "My wife..."

"Not interested."

"Huh?" I dropped my own musings and looked at her, barely missing being grabbed by those eyes.

"You called her?"

"Only five or ten times. Finally, they took the phone off the hook. Didn't answer the door either."

"You went to my house?"

"Well, you'd already been there. Bernie, you're on the inside here. I figured, if we're following you, let's go where you'd go. Got some nice video of the kids in the yard. Maybe later, you can identify which ones are Frank's, Officer Tierney's, and yours."

OMG, WTF, I thought. Jen and Betty were going to have my ears, or other lower body parts, for this. The fact that I couldn't control what other reporters do would be seen only as an excuse.

"Sure, sure, I'll make some sort of statement later," I said, defeated.

"But only to me?" She gave my upper arm a hopeful, teasing squeeze.

There was a clatter at the back of the room and all side conversations stopped as the guest of honor arrived. D.A. Carson Rittenhouse, followed by the Commissioner, entered the room, to be memorialized by still and video photogs as if they were the bride and her dad approaching the altar.

Rittenhouse went to the podium without a word and adjusted the gooseneck mike stand to his 6'3" height. Silver hair topped a patrician face. The descendant of old, old, olde Philadelphia, he'd come to his office in a three way election day collision involving a black Democrat who was barely qualified to drive and a black ambulance chaser who always referred to himself in the third person (Larry Forbes wants to be your D.A. Larry Forbes wants to shake up criminal justice. Larry Forbes needs a pronoun) and Rittenhouse who had been a Superior Court judge but gave it up to run. He'd been a long-shot light horse in a city where black was not only beautiful but powerful, yet the other two were such maroons that even Philadelphia, corrupt and contented, couldn't stomach them.

"Ladies and gentlemen," he began without self-introduction. If you didn't know who he was, you were in the wrong building. "Last night, we suffered a terrible tragedy, with the shooting death of police officer Frank Tierney. His death has been ruled a homicide and we are charging his wife, Jan M. Tierney, with a general charge of homicide. She is being held without bail, pending arraign...."

"This is a travesty!" came a shout from the rear of the room. Lisette Hanratty had dropped the paper, lowered her collar and was standing, waving a finger to punctuate. The TV cameras swung around and photogs fiddled to switch to their shotgun mikes to grab her sound. I dug in my bag for my back-up recorder, so I missed her first few words. "Jan Tierney was an abused wife, an abused police wife! Afraid and threatened, she reached out to a domestic abuse hotline last weekend!"

I looked back over at Rittenhouse who was clenching the edge of the podium as blood seeped up in his face. This news was a couple of hours old, but, in here, thrown right in the D.A.'s face, it could cause a scene. Cool.

"Ms. Hanratty," he began, softly at first, then louder. "Ms. Hanratty!" With the power of the podium and its speaker system at his back, she finally stopped, and braced for the on-camera heave-ho.

"It certainly is a surprise to see you here, although not a surprise you're involved in this case," Rittenhouse went on in his normal, slightly condescending tone. "May I ask for your cooperation? How about if I make my statement and then you can come up here and make yours? Otherwise I must ask you to leave."

Touché! Heads swung back toward her. Now she was in a pickle. To continue her tirade after such a generous offer would make her look bad, but to stand at the D.A.'s podium, flanked by him and the Commissioner would make her look as if she were cooperating, not opposing, them.

She grabbed her coat and left with a shout back over her shoulder, "I'll have more to say outside."

No one followed her. She'd wait.

The commotion died down, the cameras swung back to Rittenhouse and he made show of adjusting some documents before him, publically patient. No doubt his blue blood was boiling but sometimes there were benefits to being raised in an environment where emotions were neither seen nor heard.

"As I was saying," he resumed, "this incident has cut deeply into the Philadelphia law enforcement family. Jan Tierney has confessed, both verbally at the scene and in writing in police custody after being properly Mirandized and offered legal counsel. That she has it now," he nodded after the departed Hanratty, "will affect the way the case proceeds. The Commonwealth has filed a general charge of homicide against Jan Tierney, because we are still evaluating the circumstances of the crime. At the conclusion of our investigation, we will be more specific."

"Carson, Carson," Garrison Watts waved a reporter's notebook at the D.A. "Was this self-defense? That's what Jan's lawyer is saying."

Rittenhouse, having survived the 800-pound gorilla of interruptions, was unphased by this one. "Jan Tierney has a fractured left arm, a result, she says, of an altercation with her husband that precipitated the shooting. This is part of the web of evidence we are collecting. Once we have it all, we'll make our decision, but, and let me just say this so others can't say I didn't, it is possible that this will be ruled self-defense."

The news conference went on for another 15 minutes, mostly with newspaper reporters asking increasingly obscure questions. They were still grilling Rittenhouse on the price of tea in China or some other such crap, when we reached the point of diminishing returns. I unplugged from the mult-box and, along with the camera crews, headed for the second ring of this circus outside. As I passed through the lobby, I noticed that someone else was screening visitors from behind the glass.

Chapter Thirteen

Outside, it was both the same circus and the same clowns. The DVDVAL gals were engaged in a group gripe in the glare of camera lights. Horns continued to blare as traffic inched past and drivers no doubt thought that a little violence might come in handy right about now. Lisette Hanratty stood like Moses on the shore of the sea, ready to command its obedience. Trench-coated Civil Affairs cops huddled together, counting the minutes until retirement.

The cameras once again gathered around Hanratty and reporters jostled in front to get their mike close to her mouth in all that din. It's ironic, given its context, that this sort of interview is known as a gang-bang, but, blocked out in front by the folks who needed to see her face, Gina got close in behind her and reached an arm around. I hated this. You couldn't hear a goddam thing, much less ask a question. I could tell from the way Hanratty gestured that she was pretty excited about what she had to say, but five feet away I didn't have any idea what it was. After a minute or two, Gina's arm got tired and she switched, bumping a public radio reporter who gave her a back-off-bitch glare.

A couple people asked questions, often just to have Hanratty say something more concisely or more outrageously. Brief soundbites are good, brief and wild even better. In five minutes, it was over. TV types fled back to their vans, not just for the warmth, but to wham-bam-thank-you-ma'am a little of this for playback in their upcoming live-shot.

I huddled with Gina.

"Bottom line from inside," I said, "general charge of homicide, but it could be increased or decreased, even dropped. Jan, Mrs. Tierney, had a fractured arm, maybe from a baseball bat. How about you?"

Before she could answer, I felt a tap at my shoulder and turned to find Sarah Tilson and her photog who was powering up the light. "You promised me," she said as the light flared and the mike came up.

Talk about being on the spot. I had done this to people every day for fifteen years and had no idea of the panic that hit you.

"Was your sister-in-law being abused?" Even Gina raised her mike.

"Where did you hear that?"

Sarah gave me a disapproving look, so sexy, and I wanted to please her. "That's what Lisette Hanratty just said."

"I couldn't hear a word of it. Fill me in." I was only half-listening but half plotting how to respond. I had already heard the allegation and, having been at the crime scene, figured the scenario between Jan and Frank.

"She said Jan called the Hotline, anonymously, on Sunday. They only made the connection between her and the call after the arrest. But there's audio of it. Hanratty's getting it. I think she's jerking us off so she'll be the lead story at 11, but she says it's pretty graphic."

"Okay," I said after a moment, "Here's my comment. This all comes as quite a shock. The murder, the allegations of domestic abuse all compound the trauma of two little kids who right now are without both their mother and father."

"Do you hope they let Jan out? Should they let her out?"

"For the sake of her kids, yes, but we have to let the D.A. do his job."

"You're saying you doubt her story?" Ouch, fell right in to that one. And I noticed other cameras gathering like hyenas to a fresh kill.

"Jan is my sister-in-law. She's a lovely woman, the womb-mate of my wife, and I never have had any reason to doubt her word. That's enough, thanks."

I ducked away, hoping to get the "me" back in media by putting a little distance between myself and the madding crowd. I swung around onto Juniper Street, a one lane glorified alley that ran between the D.A.'s building and Macy's. Gina padded after me but the others returned to getting ready for the next live shot.

"Nice non-answer," she smirked. "You must really be in a pickle on this."

I sagged against the side of the building. Gina stood in front of me, arms crossed over her chest. It was noticeably darker and quieter there, almost peaceful. "Since last night, I haven't known which way is up. Jan and Frank seemed as steady as Jen and me. Not perfect, but who is? They were doing the whole "marriage is hard work" thing the way it's supposed to be done, with commitment and caring. Now, what am I supposed to think?"

"Why did she do it?"

"A baseball bat to the arm is a powerful motivation," I sighed, wondering what my motivation was at this point.

"Look, I gotta go file," said Gina and suddenly she was off, back into the waning pandemonium. Right then, I loved that wall. It seemed to be the only thing holding me up in life.

"Hey, shithead," came a voice from across the narrow street, in the shadows of a breezeway. I saw a lighter flare and a face illuminated as it sucked on a cigarette. Somebody was channeling Deep Throat, the one from All the President's Men, not the porn movie, although maybe I should have asked for a second opinion.

The tiny glow of the cigarette moved toward me and Agent Semyenovic emerged into the lesser darkness of the street. Straight out of Central Casting, he was wearing a trench coat.

When he got close, he flicked his butt at me even though he wasn't even a quarter done. I managed to dodge twice, once incoming, then again when it bounced off the wall.

"I have fucking had it with you!" he said.

"Funny, I was thinking the same thing. Don't you have cooked books to decode?"

By then he has close enough that I could smell his breath and the liquor fumes on it. "Why did you send the cops my way? Did you think that will save you? Do you think I don't know what's going on here?"

If you do, please explain it to me, I wanted to say but instead I said, "The Arson Squad needed your lead about the warehouse job."

"Let them do their own work. Warren Nash is mine." You can have him, I thought, but for once, said nothing. Semyenovic plowed on as if I were active in the conversation. "They'll get nothing, nothing from me! I am after that crooked boss of yours, and your ass is grass as well, if you get in my way."

Okay, at this point, I was officially creeped out. The FBI agents I had met were all no-nonsense, button-down types and, twice in two days, this guy was all-nonsense and a few buttons short of a shirt. Of course, the agents I knew were on their best behavior at news conferences and the like and this guy was probably both off-duty and off the reservation.

"Fine!" I snapped. "Do your best, or worst! He's got lawyers who'll keep you busy until you're in the G-Man nursing home. You want to make trouble for me, take a number. The threat of you arresting me for some piss-ant crime is nothing compared to the meltdown my family is going through. Cry me a fucking river."

He backed away from my venom and I expected he'd come back at me double for speaking up. But, instead, he mellowed. Suddenly, he was all conciliatory, slapping me on the shoulder. "Yeah, that's too bad," he said.

Agent Semyenovic took a step back to reload a cigarette. I took my cue and began to walk back toward the fading fury of the demonstration. "You know, I think this case is about to crack wide open."

That's not the only thing about to crack, I thought, but kept on walking.

Although Gina was gone, there were still plenty of media types around. The live-trucks were sealed up as reporters edited their Sony sandwich packages for the next news cycle. Curiosity tickled enough that I wondered how much my mug would be featured, but I flicked open my cell phone and called Carrie with the inside story, presuming Gina was doing the outside.

"I can be live with you at 5:30," I offered and Carrie agreed. "Then I'll have Memorex and a couple of cuts by 6:00."

"You're working late, aren't you? Why not go live at 6, too? Let's at least be as current as the TV's."

"Sure, fine," I replied without much enthusiasm. Doing live-shots like this was show biz, nothing more. With the news conference and demonstration over, there was simply no longer anything that couldn't be recorded.

"See you at 5:30," Carrie chirped and hung up. Must be close to an eBay auction deadline.

There was no reason to stay there in the cold, I figured, so I dodged through the still gridlocked traffic and reversed my route to the car.

By 5:30, I had a cut of Rittenhouse cued up and ready for my live-shot, which consisted of listening to cue-back of WPN over the cell phone, talking a little bit to introduce the quote, holding the phone microphone to the recorder speaker as it played and then a line out and a sign off from me. That left me listening to the station again and normally I would have hung up in a snap to get back to my work, but evening anchor Sam Hancock was already setting up Carrie's follow-up report on the demonstration. I hung on and listened.

"....heated demonstration in the cold outside the D.A's office. WPN's Gina Ginelli has more..."

Her voice began with natural sound of the demonstration in the background. "A couple dozen activists from the Delaware Valley Domestic Violence Action League shouted and paraded, protesting the murder charge even before it was officially announced. Defense attorney Lisette Hanratty, fresh from making a scene inside the D.A.'s office, laid it on the line outside."

Next was Hanratty bellowing, the part I couldn't hear for all the racket earlier. "This is way beyond a miscarriage of justice! It's an impeachable offense to charge a battered woman with defending herself!"

Gina's voice resumed: "Jan Tierney, who suffered a fractured arm, is accused of shooting her police officer husband to death during what appears to have been a violent domestic clash Tuesday night. Her brother-in-law, our own Bernie Gaston, was at the murder scene..."

Then my own voice: "A baseball bat to the arm is a powerful motivation."

Gina again: "but for self-defense, or murder, only time will tell. Gina Ginelli, WPN."

I don't think I actually heard her lockout because my mind was racing off. WTF, that wasn't what I'd said to the media scrum. I replayed my conversation with Gina in the side street. I had been leaning against the wall. She'd come up, her arms across her chest, and the microphone in one hand. Damn her, she'd had it on! She punked me, played on our friendship, our collegiality. What the hell else did I say when I didn't know she was recording?

I thumped my head on the steering wheel. Okay, I thought, now things have really gone to hell.

Of course, that was before I went home.

Chapter Fourteen

It was probably 8:15 by the time I dragged myself out of the car in front of my domicile. It hadn't taken me long to file my tonight stories or tomorrow's, since I knew the facts so well. Bim, bam, boom, I was outta there. I tried calling Gina to give her a piece of my mind but she must have known I would and didn't pick up. Not that it mattered. I could hear the non-existent conversation in my head.

"You recorded me without my permission."

"It was a continuation of the interview ten seconds earlier."

"Your microphone was hidden."

"No, it was in plain sight. True, I didn't stick it up under your nose, but there was no need. It was quieter."

"You betrayed me."

"Get over yourself. You're now a news source, a public figure for the duration of this story. People want to know your opinion, although God only knows why, since you're being such a priss about it."

See? Why bother?

I let myself in to find the four kids doing their version of pro rasslin' in the living room. All that was missing was the make-up and a breakaway chair. They were howling with laughter, throwing themselves onto one another with abandon as I peeled off my boots. Betty sat nearby on a couch, pretending at least to read a magazine, waiting for the other howl that was sure to come when one kid's idea of fun turned into another's idea of pain.

"Hey," I said, interrupting the melee.

"Daddy!" screamed my two and they launched themselves for my legs. Clamp, clamp, and they were trying to knock me over. I didn't take the bait, but pried Elizabeth off to give her a quick kiss and then Lorraine. Sam and Frankie lay panting against the couch on either side of Grandma's feet.

"How are you guys doing?" I asked them as neutrally as I could.

"I miss Mommy," said Frankie, suddenly sniffly.

"Now, now," said Betty, scooping him up. "We've had enough of that already. You can be a big boy and stay up a little longer or a little boy and go to bed right now."

Frankie considered it for a moment, a bit defiant. I thought he actually might drive down Tantrum Highway, but he folded his cards with a sag of his shoulders and a whimper. "Big boy," he said.

I walked their way, towseling his hair as I bent to sweep Samantha off the floor. "How are you, angel?" She looked at me with her dark eyes, unusual in this family. The truth was, I liked that kid a lot. Frank Jr bore the burden of his name. "Little" Frank. Chip off the old block or blockhead as I sometimes knew Frank to have been. Samantha, though, was sweet, smart and cooperative. You could actually have a conversation with her, because she was interested in the world, not just the nearest toy.

Tonight, though, she mumbled only a halfhearted "Okay" and who could blame her? I still didn't know what she had seen last night, or Frankie for that matter, but even if they'd walked through the room with paper bags over their heads there was enough potential trauma to go around.

I put her down. "Betty, how are you?" She looked at me as if I had suddenly become a Baby Ruth floating in the pool.

"Go see Jen in the back," she said stiffly. "I'll hold down the fort out here."

I didn't need a welling up of somber music to know that I wasn't in for hugs and kisses from the Mrs. After hanging up my coat, I entered the lioness' den.

"Hey, hon," I began. Jen looked up from the table where she sat with the handset from our cordless phone. It looked as if she had been crying, or drinking, or both.

"Are you trying to fuck this up?" Her profanity shocked me and reset the Bernie's-in-Trouble-meter into the Red Zone.

"What do you mean?" I asked, although I suspected.

"I can't believe what you're saying on the TV. You don't know Jan didn't do it? You don't know!?!" Her voice rose into something that you'd hear from a snake that had been kicked in the balls. Okay, I thought, no nookie tonight, unless it's make-up sex, and even that's going to take some doing.

"No," I said, "I don't. I know she's your twin and you're closer than Frick and Frack but you weren't there and neither was I. All I said was, let the D.A. do his job. Is that too much to ask?"

'That's exactly what Bernie Gaston, media talking head, should say, but not Bernie Gaston, family member. Bernie Gaston, family member, should be out there with that loudmouth lawyer. Boy, is she a piece of work? You should grab a protest sign and get Jan out of jail! She's the injured one! He's the bastard who got just what he deserved!"

We had visited Niagara Falls the summer before all this happened, mostly because it's the kind of thing you do with kids. We were in this park on the edge of the Niagara River upstream from the Falls, and Jen and the girls were playing in the shallows. I was standing on the shore, waiting for one of them to be swept up in a swirl of current and carried toward doom. Then, the breath of disaster was on my neck, so palpable, that I stood as tense as a sprinter waiting for the starting gun, until I suggested wading time was over.

I was having another such moment there in the kitchen.

As much to give myself time to think as a place to sit, I pulled out a chair and plunked down next to Jen. I glanced at her injured ankle and saw she had it in an air cast, finally. "Talk to me," I said gently. "What's going on here? Did you know about this abuse?"

Instead of answering, Jen lurched to her feet and hobbled over to close two French doors that connected the back of the house to the front. When she sat, she continued in a subdued tone of voice.

"They'd been having trouble for weeks, maybe months. I don't want to go into gory details. What you don't know you can't say on TV." Ouch. "But Jan confided in me that Frank had been passed over for a promotion and was not exactly despondent but pretty damn pissed. I think there had been some shoving, certainly a lot of arguments, but last night..... Last night, it just all blew up."

I had a million questions, but none seemed likely to get me out of the doghouse. So I sat silently for a moment?

"Have you talked with Jan? How's she holding up?"

Jen shook her head sadly. "I can't get in to see her until tomorrow after they move her from the Roundhouse to prison." She sniffled slightly. I wondered if that "do you want to be big?" routine would work on her. "Then I can go in for visiting hours. The lawyer says she's fine, though. I gave her my cell number because you press people won't leave us alone and I don't dare answer the house phone. This is the first time all day this thing," as she wagged the cordless handset, "has stopped ringing."

"Well, you did the right thing," I responded lamely. I was hoping that a little generic reassurance would take the heat off me, since, after all, I couldn't even control the people I worked with, much less the rival stations' personnel.

Jen sighed. "The worst part is Sam and Frankie. They're asking, when can Mommy come home? And all I can tell them is, soon, I hope."

It's a genetic defect, I'm sure, that I am simply incapable of shutting up. It comes in handy in my line of work, but sitting there at the table I should never have said:

"I didn't get the computer back yet, but I will, first thing in the morning."

Her face darkened. She rapped the bottom end of the phone on the table sharply, but all she said was, "Make sure you do."

I left the table and returned to the front of the house for some kid time. My two were pestering Betty about resuming the wrestling but Sam and Frank Jr. were now subdued. They sat together in an armchair, Samantha making a great show of reading a magazine to her little brother. Her narration was top-notch although she was making almost all of it up.

I fooled around with Elizabeth and Lorraine for a moment until they too wanted a book read. I went to the kids' "library", which was a teetering pile in the corner, about half on and half off a thrift store bookcase, and pulled out something that had to do with children shaped like fruits going to school.

Betty ceded the couch to us and the cousins, their "reading" forgotten, joined my kids in cuddling up, each leaning in as needed to get a look at the pages. There were all sorts of fruits representing your standard-issue ethnic rainbow of people. They lined up behind Teacher Tomato for a field trip to the zoo, each perky peach, punk plum and cornrowed kiwi spouting bromides about cooperation and kindness to animals. It was pretty dreadful, but there wasn't a literary critic among my audience of four.

I turned the page to show them getting on the bus. Its driver Bob Banana was wearing a uniform of sorts, looking something like Ralph Kramden of the Honeymooners if he'd been raised by Dole.

"Daddy!" said Frankie, smacking his finger on Bob. Samantha looked away in disgust and Lorraine began squirming out of her spot. Before I could continue, she had walked across the room, plucked another book from the stack and returned to plunk it on top of the one I held. This precipitated a round of tired-kid bickering that degenerated quickly into squalling and tears. Betty scooped up Lorraine and Frankie with practiced grace and, despite their squirming and histrionics, carted them upstairs.

"That went well, " I said to no one in particular, but Samantha looked at me gravely, shook her head slowly and intoned with all the gravitas that a five year old can muster:

"Little kids. They just never learn."

I thought I was going to bust a gut. Like I said, Samantha's all right.

Chapter Fifteen: Thursday

    I got a decent night's sleep for once and was puttering around the kitchen scrambling some eggs when the phone rang. Jen answered and handed it to me without comment. It sure was chilly in the doghouse.

    "Yeah," I said, basking in the glow of my wife's disapproval.

    "Beanie." It was Silcox. I knew I had to get an unlisted number. "We need you at an 9:00 thing near Norristown." I looked at the wall clock. It was 7:49.

    "It'll be tight," I replied without the "you stupid fuck" that I attached mentally. Norristown was at least 45 minutes away, even if the Turnpike wasn't gridlocked.

    "Do your best. There's a preliminary hearing at the West Norriton DJ's office, a drunk driving fatal from last month. Speeding drunk slams into two young lovers pulling out of a church. He lives, they don't. It's a movie of the week."

    I sighed. "Where is it?" Silcox rattled off the address of the District Justice courtroom and I hung up.

Jen looked at me coolly from across her coffee mug. "Leaving so soon?"

"Come on," I implored. "This is what pays the bills. I have to go to court. It could start at 9 or 10 or tomorrow at 3:15. It'll probably take no more than 5 minutes but if I'm not there I'll miss the sound."

I had to dash. I grabbed my keys, coat and a kiss (all right, a peck on her chilly cheek) before I hit the road. A quick check of the traffic report found that, yes, there were significant delays westbound on the Turnpike near Fort Washington so my bottleneck was already in place. I tried not to watch the minutes evaporate on the dashboard clock and focus my attention on the bumper ahead of me. Once I got off at Norristown, I pulled over for a moment to check a map book stashed on the passenger side. Sure, somebody might have a GPS system, but that somebody might actually have a company car.

The District Justice's office was a few miles away in largely unfamiliar terrain. Even though I'd worked in the Philly area for five years, much of it was unexplored. I think I'd been to the Montgomery County courthouse in Norristown twice and out to a community meeting bitching about the Limerick nuclear power plant once. Other than that, we did a lot of suburban coverage by phone.

As I pulled up to the DJ's digs, I could see that the shindig was ready to start. Several TV trucks were in place and I eased in to a parking space nearby. Grabbing my gear bag, I joined the media phalanx in front of a squat nondescript brick building.

"Hey, Bernie," said Carlos, a TV shooter who I saw more than now and then. "You made it for the perp walk." He powered up his camera and adjusted the weight on his shoulder.

Perp, or perpetrator, walks are a staple of TV news but are only occasionally interesting on radio. The sound of a suspect walking by is generally like the sound of one hand clapping but every so often the bad guy freaks at seeing the cameras and starts yelling obscenities or blasphemies or recipes. Who cares? As long as it's a reaction, we can bleep the hell out of it, or bleep the bleep out of it.

A county prison van pulled slowly into the parking lot and swung around, so its rear doors faced us. Two huge deputies each with a gun, nightstick, mace canisters and game-face scowl climbed out of the front and walked to the back. TV cameramen maneuvered into an arc to get the best view as the driver flipped through a jangling wad of keys for the right one. I hit "record" and raised my mic as the deputies helped a skinny white guy in shackles and an orange jumpsuit out of the van.

Less like a desperado and more like a pimple-faced high school dropout who's just been bitch-slapped by reality, he stared wide-eyed at the cameras as he was ushered into the building. Sometimes, when they feel kind, authorities might allow a suspect a little dignity and toss a coat or sweater over his or her head, especially with someone who might not even be an adult in the eyes of the law. Not this time, though, and that said volumes about how seriously this case was being taken.

That may even have dawned on this mope when he saw the TV's and from deep within his web of denial came the news flash; you're in a heap of trouble, jocko. But he kept his mouth shut and I was left with nothing. I put my recorder back in my bag and followed the parade of reporters inside.

The cameras stayed outside because Pennsylvania does not allow them in court nor, truth be told, recording devices so technically I was breaking the law just by going in while "packing". Most of the time, though, since I would not actually record in the courtroom, and since a little place like this didn't have a contraband holding area, shh, don't ask, don't tell.

What surprised me in the courtroom, a Spartan layout beggared by the sets of those Ask-Judge-So-and-So shows on TV, was how many people sat in its folding chairs in the gallery area. I noticed Garrison Watts whispering to an African-American woman in the front row who, like about twenty others, was adorned with a three-inch button presenting a portrait of the dead couple. Displays like that were increasingly popular among aggrieved families and could prompt a trial judge to order them removed, lest the jury be swayed.

The suspect was taken through a low swinging gate into the business area of the courtroom and plunked in a chair by a desk. The deputies removed his handcuffs and he rubbed his wrists as a man in a dark suit, already there, leaned over and conversed with him in low tones. I found a seat near the family members and was about to strike up a conversation when there was a whoosh of air as the door to the atrium opened. A wiry Latino in a pinstripe suit tailored to NASA tolerances strode into the room as if there were springs in his shoes.

Oh, my, I thought. Pedro Calderon, probably the county's top homicide prosecutor. This kid didn't know it but the TV cameras were the least of his worries. With Calderon on the case, the death penalty would be on the table if it could be.

Once Calderon had shaken hands with the opposing attorney and taken a seat at the other table up front, a bailiff leaned through a side door. Then he turned back to us and announced, "All rise. This District Court of the Commonwealth of Pennsylvania under the honorable District Justice John Henning is now in session. Cease all conversations and turn off all phones and electronics."

Henning swept into the room like something out of Sleepy Hollow, a gaunt, spectral face trailing black robes. All he needed was a scythe.

"Be seated," he said once he was behind his bench. "What's our first case today?"

The bailiff handed him a clipboard at which he glanced before peering sharply over at the defendant. "And who have we here?"

The man in the suit stood next to the defendant. "Clayton Morrissey representing Richard Taub, your honor."

"Ah, Mr. Morrissey. It's early in the year. Getting a head start on pro bono work?"

"No, your honor, I have been retained by the Taub family." Hmm, I thought as I begin to scribble in my notepad, a gold-plated perp. In the city, especially at preliminary hearings, it was often a public defender putting in a desultory appearance. Prelims were usually the first time anyone got a good look at the prosecution's case. It was so rare any counts were dismissed that unless the case was controversial or emotional, like this one, it hardly paid to go.

Calderon stood up. "First Assistant District Attorney Pedro Calderon for the Commonwealth, your Honor. Mr. Taub is charged in the wrongful deaths of two teenagers, Isaiah Wilson and Jasmine Thiel, a couple of 17 year olds. This is a heinous, senseless crime compounded by Mr. Taub's intoxication."

The DJ held up his hand. "Save it for the jury, Mr. Calderon." He looked at the clipboard. "You're really charging him with third degree murder?"

"Yes, your honor. The depraved indifference of this case has moved it beyond any ordinary homicide by vehicle."

"Okay, okay. Mr. Morrissey, I take it you will be arguing..."

"That this goes way beyond what the statute allows."

"Before we get to arguments, how about some evidence?"

Calderon shared a glance with Morrissey, then said. "Counsel have agreed that for the purposes of this preliminary hearing, several things will be stipulated." "Stipulated" is legalese for "we agree on that". "Among those are that the victims, Wilson and Thiel, died on the evening of December 23rd, that the accident occurred on Trooper Rd. at the entrance to Grace Cathedral Church, that Mr. Taub was the driver of a vehicle heading north at a high rate of speed when the crash occurred, and that Mr. Taub was legally intoxicated."

"You agree to all this?" the DJ wondered, aiming a stare at Morrissey.

"For the purposes of today's hearing, yes. To speed things along."

"There's quite a bit of physical evidence from the accident investigation," said Calderon. "These things are not really in doubt."

"So what is in doubt?" Henning wanted to know.

"The charge, your honor, as you indicated yourself," Morrissey answered. "Third degree murder is absurd."

"Two young lovers were killed!" Calderon barked.

"And they helped, at least Mr. Wilson did," Morrissey replied evenly. A gasp went through the gallery and the woman next to me fumbled with her purse to extract a tissue.

"Outrageous!" Calderon snapped.

"At ease." The DJ made a calm-yourself wave of his hand. "That's a bold contention, Mr. Morrissey. Explain."

"Let us assume for purposes of this hearing that Mr. Taub was drunk and speeding along Trooper Rd. at 65 or 70 miles an hour. Let us assume that his car t-boned the car driven by the victim Isaiah Wilson pulling out of the church, killing Mr. Wilson and his girlfriend Ms. Thiel. If, as we are assuming for these purposes only, Mr. Taub was no longer capable of the judgment necessary to drive, he cannot have had enough indifference for it to be depraved."

"You're saying because he's drunk he's not responsible?" The judge's question brought a new round of gasps and sobs.

"I'm saying he's not solely responsible. Keep in mind, Your Honor, Mr. Taub's car did not crash through a house, just minding its own business off on the side of the road. It did not hit a car stopped for a traffic light nor veer into oncoming traffic. Mr. Taub was actually in his assigned lane when Mr. Wilson pulled out in front of him. The Commonwealth says Mr. Taub was drunk. What was Mr. Wilson's excuse?"

"Wha?????" exploded in the gallery and everyone turned to see a silver-haired African-American church-lady type, the one Garrison Watts had been chatting up earlier, wringing her eyes into a handkerchief. I couldn't tell if it had been a question, a wail or both. Others around her muttered in a rising tide.

"Order, order," said Henning, punctuated with gavel whacks. "This is an emotional case, to be sure, but any more outbursts and I'll clear the courtroom."

Those nearby tried to comfort, or at least quiet, the woman. Reporters wrote furiously and made plans to revisit the issue with her later.

"You honor," Calderon said, trying to be business-like but anger clearly lurked. "This is outrageous. It is blaming the victim. Mr. Wilson could not have known how impaired the on-coming driver was."

"But he could have seen the on-coming car," the DJ noted conversationally. "He should have seen it. Then he would not have pulled out in front of it and Mr. Taub might have hit someone else." Henning flicked his eyes toward Morrissey, daring him to say anything. There was a moment of silence as the judge considered. "What's bail here?"

"No bail, your honor," Calderon said immediately, "and the Commonwealth requests that be continued. Two people have died.

"I'm aware of that, counselor, very aware. Mr. Taub, how old are you?"

"Twenty-two, sir."

"You have a job or go to school?"

"Job, sir, at least I had. I don't know if it will still be there, after this."

"Do you live at home?"

"Yes, sir, with my parents. I saw them in the back as I came in."

"Mr. and Mrs. Taub, would you please come up to the railing?" A man and a woman not yet 50 rose from the last row of spectator chairs and ambled forward. When they arrived at the little gate, Henning went on, "If I grant him bail, there is one iron-clad rule. He cannot drive. No, two rules. He cannot drink alcohol either. One would think that after something like this, that could go without saying but no. There, I have said it."

"Your honor," Calderon began to protest.

Henning held up his palm. "I am dismissing the third degree murder counts but holding the defendant for trial on everything else. I am setting bail at $150,000, 10 percent cash, and setting an arraignment date of," he looked at a desk calendar in front of him, "March 22nd at the Courthouse. Mr. Taub, you'll be getting a summons with the time and courtroom on it.

"Mr. and Mrs. Taub, do you agree with this? He can't drive. You'll have to take him around like he's 15 again. He can't drink, not a drop, although maybe a swig of communion wine would do him good."

"We're Jewish," said Mr. Taub.

"Then go easy on the Mogen David," said Henning. "Do you agree?"

"Yes," they said in unison.

"Deputies, you will retain custody of the defendant and return him to the county prison until such a time as bail is posted. I think we're done here." He rapped his gavel and exited stage right. There would be other cases later but, given the crowd and the controversy, he'd powder his nose or something while the room cleared.

There was stunned silence for a moment. The Taubs reached over the railing, trying to touch and reassure their son, but the deputies slapped the cuffs back on him and hauled him out of the room.

We electronic media guys fled in a pack, the TV reporters to alert their photogs that it was time for the main event, and me to stake out a position beside them in search of sound. A couple of newspaper reporters tried to buttonhole the lawyers but the victims' families stormed outside, boiling mad. There were unmistakable wails and howls of dismay now, caught on tape by us First Amendment voyeurs. We got wide shots and natural sound of the small fry, but when I saw Watts move toward the church lady I knew it was time. Microphones sprouted like mushroom caps.

"Mrs. Wilson, Mrs. Wilson, you lost your son in that horrible accident and now the defense seems to be blaming him."

She looked startled, impaled by the unblinking electronic eyes and held up on both sides by younger relatives. "What's your reaction," Watts prodded. "How does it feel?"

"It feels like hell!" she snapped. "My boy didn't do nothin' wrong but go to church and love the Lord Jesus. He and that sweet girl of his was comin' out of choir practice, choir practice! when they was run down like dogs. Is that what my son is to that judge, a dog?"

I'm thinking, money cut, money cut, take it to the bank.

Mama Wilson suddenly whirled to me. "You there. I seen you on TV last night. First they askin' you questions on TV, now you here bothering me to put me on TV. Which side are you on, boy?" I could have responded that I was going to put her on radio not TV, but that seemed beside the point.

Watts or someone else poked her with another question, what did she think about the District Justice, and she launched into a tirade that he ought to be horsewhipped. This was an embarrassment of riches.

While most of our attention was on Mrs. Wilson, Morrissey tried to make a break for it. He slipped out the front door sideways and headed casually toward the parking lot.

I saw him and so did some of the victims' family members. "There he is!" one yelled and in an instant he was surrounded by hecklers. Photogs encircled the circle, some hoisting their still or video gear up over their heads to get a look down inside the jostling.

A large man pushed Morrissey with an open hand. "It'll be your fault if you get in the way of my fist."

Mrs. Wilson waded in and smacked him with her handbag just before the deputies and a couple of township cops charged to the rescue. Morrissey scurried off to his car, pursued by the camera guys. He seemed disinclined to stick around to comment. I could call him later, in the safety of his office, unless his staff was beating him up too.

Calderon emerged and was, if anything, more energized than when he'd entered. He waved Mrs. Wilson and a couple of other family members over for a brief private conversation. Then he strode toward the cameras and paused while we got ourselves in order. He didn't even wait for us to ask a question.

"What just happened in there is unacceptable! Despite Justice Henning's decision, the Commonwealth intends to seek third degree murder charges against Mr. Taub and we will re-file those charges, this time with a judge of the Court of Common Pleas in Norristown."

"Will you file today?" someone asked.

"Yes, but it's doubtful that a hearing can be scheduled on such short notice. That means that unless the Taub family is without the means to post the $15,000 cash District Justice Henning required, the younger Taub, behind the wheel during a double fatal traffic accident, will be back out on the streets."

"Well, not exactly, Pedro," Watts chimed in. "He can't drive, can't party under the judge's order."

"But he'll be free, Gary, while two young victims are dead."

"Will a third degree murder charge bring them back?"

"Of course not," Calderon bristled, "but it will go a long way toward tipping the scales of justice back to where they should be. We do not have a law in Pennsylvania that treats drunk driving and certainly drunk driving fatalities with the seriousness they deserve. Failing that we persuade the Legislature to craft a new law, we have to use the law already on the books. If this isn't depraved indifference, I don't know what is. Thank you all."

Calderon twisted himself out of the media cordon and stalked toward his car. Obviously, we hadn't heard the last of this.

The TV guys spied the Taubs and pursued them but I thought that was piling on. What were they going to say, we love our son? Beep, beep, beep, this just in.

Anyway, I was full up on facts and sound, so it was time to file.

As I sat in my car, porting voicecuts and natural sound into the laptop, honing and crafting the story (the first version was 58 seconds so I had some editing to do before sending it in), my mind kept coming back to what Mrs. Wilson had to say: whose side was I on?

While I certainly could understand her point (I more than anyone else within earshot of it), it struck me as unfair. If we weren't there to hear her complain, or to witness to the DJ's dismissal of the most serious charge, I knew damn well that these same people would be bitching that we didn't care about them because they're black. I can hear her scolding us, "Big white media don't care 'bout little black folks 'les we robbing a bank."

There is, of course, some truth to that, (we care more about anyone who robs a bank) but it ignores the bigger truth that we can only do so much. News, even on CNN or FNC, was a tiny snapshot of what's going on and when you covered one story you were ignoring lots of others. Life was simply too big and complex to fit even in a 24 hour news wheel.

Yet, especially after what Gina had done, I knew what it felt like to have reporters step on my emotional toes without even so much as a generic "sorry." No doubt, the Tierneys were wrestling with this very issue, bruised by the loss of Frank and the circumstances, and uncertain how to react to the media spotlight, both unwelcome and unavoidable.

Finally finished with the wrap and a couple of cuts each of Mrs. Wilson and A.D.A. Calderon, I did what any good journalist would do, chose not to think about it any more.

Chapter Sixteen

I called in to the newsroom after uploading the story. Silcox answered agitatedly. I asked him what the problem was.

"TBC is on the rag. This FBI thing has him pretty rattled. He was just back here looking for you, chewing up the scenery, pacing like he's already an inmate. Christ, I don't think I've seen him back here in, what, six months and now it's twice in one morning."

"I feel your pain," I responded, mentally adding, Good, you deserve more, you putz. "But what's up next for me? Any more assignments?"

I heard some computer clicks and he said, "Not right now, but you got two messages, one from Mark Solarz, something about MLK day. Isn't this the guy I told you to call on Monday? What the fuck is it with PR loads? We gotta do things on their schedule?" Duh. "The other is from somebody Tierney. Is this about your brother-in-law? Maybe it's news."

"Well, it's news to me, pal. Which Tierney?"

"Doesn't say, but here's the phone number." Silcox rattled off a number in the 610 area code, the western suburbs. I didn't recognize it since I'd had very little contact with the Tierney clan. Once the funeral was over, I would probably have even less. I thanked Silcox and told him I'd mosey on in once I'd called the Tierneys.

I dialed the number and it turned out to be a law office with one of those automated directories. I punched in T-I-E-R-N-E-Y and was connected to Lawrence Tierney, Frank's younger brother, who picked up after a couple of rings.

"Hi, this is Bernie Gaston. You called me."

"Yes, yes," he responded and I could hear the shuffling of papers.

"Look, I'm real sorry about Frank. I was there the other night, after it happened."

"We saw you on TV last night." His voice was a tad colder. "Please do not presume to speak for Frank's family."

"I wouldn't and don't think I did." I was thinking, how the hell many people saw the news last night? What'd they do, record it? Put it up on YouTube? I'd been scolded twice already that morning and once last night about my brief appearance as spokesvictim. Maybe I should have combed my hair or something. "I could only speak from my perspective. Is that what you called about, to critique my soundbite?"

"No, but that colors what I'm about to say. My Mom and Dad would appreciate... " He stretched out the word as if unsure it was the right one, "if you'd not come to the funeral. They are upset enough." He was beginning to pick up steam. "Since your wife looks just like Frank's killer and you, well, you seem to be on her side...."

"All I said was the D.A. should do his job."

"My brother never laid a hand on her!" Now we were getting to the nitty gritty. "That's a goddamn lie and I ought to sue you all for defamation."

"She has a broken arm! For Chrissakes, Larry, I don't blame you for being upset, but what'd she do, hit herself? Just to pretend domestic violence so she could get arrested? Shit, if she was just going to kill him, she'd come up with something better than that!"

"My big brother is dead, goddamn it, and I don't want to hear any shit about it! Just stay away, please. Leave us to our grief."

"Sure, sure," I answered quickly, trying to reduce the tone of the call a couple of DEFCON levels. "Larry, Jen and I have nothing but sorrow over this. We won't do a thing to make it worse. You'll be in our prayers." Right then, I was praying for cell call dropout.

He sighed loudly. "I'm sorry to take this out on you. I am so pissed off at Jan, so pissed. I'm trying to keep busy so I don't think, because when I think, it's about Frank and me doing this and that as kids. Down the shore fishing, at school where he protected me from bullies. Once he actually jammed a guy's head into an open locker and slammed the door on him. Now he's gone and it's her fault."

I kept my silence, wondering if he'd continue but he finally said, "Look, I don't mean to be offensive but no parent should have to bury a child, even an adult child. Maybe send my Mom and Dad a nice card."

"Give them my sympathies, Larry. Frank was always busting on me but he was a good guy. Take care."

"You too, Jimmy Olsen, you too." Another comedian. It ran in the family.

I clicked off and looked down at the laptop on the passenger seat. That triggered a thought: the computer! Yes, yes, I can get out of the doghouse!

I hit Oliver's number and he picked up on the third ring. "Silicon Rally Computer Repairs. You break it, we'll take it. Oliver speaking. "

"Oliver, Bernie Gaston. How's it going?"

"Ah, fine, Bern, fine." It didn't sound fine, but I bulled on heedlessly. I'd had enough heart-to-hearts for the day.

"Listen, about that computer I dropped off, forget about it. My wife went all PMS on me about how it was supposed to be thrown out, not repaired. I don't know why she'd even bother taking the thing from her sister rather than dumping it in the trash." My frustration was showing but Oliver, ever the geek, put in:

"You really shouldn't send them to the landfill. They're full of all sorts of bad stuff. This one is full of bad stuff."

"Well, do with it whatever you do. Reduce, reuse, recycle and I'll pay you for your time."

"No - no problem, Bernie. We'll straighten it out later."

"Great. Thanks. See you," I disconnected and tucked the phone in my pocket, feeling relieved for the first time that day. See you later, doghouse.

The drive back to the station was largely by autopilot. I skirted Conshohocken to avoid the traffic and slid into the station parking lot with hardly a second thought. Something caught my eye at the far end of the warehouse lot, a dark car idling, its tailpipe putting out a small cloud of condensing exhaust.

Trucks came in and out of there all the time but cars were pretty much restricted to the staff and none of us would park at the other end of the pavement, much less idling.

I entered the building by the back door and almost ran into Silcox on his way out. "Carrie has something for you," he said as he rushed to daylight like a miner who had been trapped for a week.

I plopped into "my seat" in the newsroom and fiddled with emails while Carrie pretended to be blocking out Hank's next cut-in but I noticed the eBay logo on the screen.

Seeing the message from Marc Solarz, I decided, what the hell, let's finally get this thing out of the way but only heard his voicemail once again. It was like Groundhog Day but without the laughs. I left a more polite message but I think the sentiment got through: the ball's in your court, hoser.

Carrie finally paid me a moment's attention, handing me a sheet of paper. "Councilwoman Doros is having a thing at 12:30 about her neighborhood redevelopment bill. She's got some real estate investors in her sights." Oh no, I thought, don't tell me, but one look at her press release and I was sure my karma needed to go in the shop. Doros was going to bitch about the Rosen-Philadelphia Real Estate Investment Trust, the one that the FBI agent thought had some connection to the arson job, the one in which TBC was an investor.

"This is a little awkward," I told Carrie. "Can't Gina do this?"

"She's anchoring tonight and I have no one else."

"Shit."

"What's the problem? You got a thing for Doros?" Councilwoman Elizabeth Doros was a striking Puerto Rican of maybe 40 well-lived years. She favored tight skirts, bright red lipstick and nails, and earrings about the size of chandeliers. She spoke with a pronounced, some said cultivated, Spanish accent and had been known to go all fiery Latina on anyone who crossed her. She seemed, incredibly enough in Philadelphia, honest inasmuch as she lobbied relentlessly for tax breaks and whatever else government could do to bring jobs into the barrio. REITs really fried her chorizo because they represented faceless Anglo money leveraging her people off the ladder of upward mobility to gentrify (read: make whiter) places where other, darker folks had struggled for years.

So, did I have a thing for her? Could be, but that was beside the point. I had so many conflicts of interest here that I was going to need U.N. peacekeepers.

"Sure, fine, whatever," I said in abject surrender. I looked at the press release. 12:30 at her office on North Broad Street. At least it wasn't City Hall for once. I'd been there so much they'd be charging me rent.

"Well, if it isn't Deep Throat," said a gravelly voice. I turned to find Hank O'Hare standing in the studio door, swimming pool-sized coffee mug in his hand. It was probably time for a drain and fill. "You know, Bern, back when I was in Buffalo," which was when news was delivered by smoke signal, "we had a guy who was on the hook to the mob. Every time he was out at a crime story, he had to check in with the capo to make sure it wasn't one of their operations. Eventually, they found him face-down in the Niagara River."

"Hank, go back in your room," I said.

"Nope, gotta drain the dragon first," and winking at Carrie, "although at my age maybe I could use some help."

"I'll loan you my tweezers," Carrie said, barely looking up.

"You young people have no respect." Hank let the studio door swing shut behind him.

"You old people don't deserve any."

This could and would go on all day. I slipped out before knives and brass knuckles appeared. It wasn't really as nasty as it sounded although the Human Resources department, if we had had one, would have been scandalized. Hank was just Hank. He'd been an FM disk jockey back when that was synonymous with doper and had chosen his name because it sounded risqué and was better than Walter Bielowicz, which was what appeared on his Social Security card and other secret documents.

The thought of Carrie, Hank and tweezers was distracting as I got into my Honda, but when I shifted from reverse to drive I noticed that car again in my rearview mirror, and it seemed to be moving toward me. I hit the gas a little harder than usual and leaped from the parking lot out onto the street. A car honked, not at me, but the dark car as it merged with almost wreck-ful disregard.

I was not panicked, just bemused. It was probably that loony FBI agent or one of his hench-agents. My tax dollars at work, but the question was, why? I'd already given my deposition. Presumably, if I'd said something wrong they could arrest me, or if they wanted more information they could just subpoena me again. So tailing me might only be to make me nervous, make me do something stupid, and let me tell you, I was just the guy for the job.

I decided to shake my tail and he, behind tinted windows in that non-descript sedan, shook right back. At first, I just took some unusual turns, slowed to try to time traffic lights so that I could make a left and leave him stranded. He didn't care, just punched it through on yellow, red, didn't matter. Presumably, if a cop caught him, he'd flash a badge and resume the chase. Maybe there was even a second car out there, although my lengthy experience with cop shows and Dirty Harry movies was that the whole idea of the tag team was to remain undetected. The horse was out of the barn on this one.

I killed about ten minutes doing loop-de-loops through Conshohocken then decided to see how he did on the Schuylkill. This was stupid and arrogant of me. As I slipped onto the highway from one of its maddening uphill ramps and fifty foot merge lanes, a truck blasted its horn and came within inches of having a new hood ornament. I glanced in the wing mirrors to see the dark car move in behind the truck. We lumbered on for a mile or so, trapped in a heavy metal dance line, until traffic began to speed up and pull apart. The dark car darted into the left lane but became stuck behind a pokey-po who had no business being there.

Serves you right, I thought, and eyed the upcoming Green Lane exit but just as I was about to take it, the dark car made a move on the left to where I could almost see its driver through the smoky windshield. With no turn signal, I cut right a little early for the ramp and slammed on the brakes sending up a cloud of dirt and gravel in the narrow shoulder. The truck horn bellowed angrily as the dark car did a spontaneous lane change onto the ramp nearly locking bumpers.

I hit the gas and swerved back onto the expressway. There was a horn-section symphony behind me and if my pursuer hadn't noticed I wasn't on the ramp ahead of him the sound surely told him where I was. I darted left and tried to hide behind the big rig but almost immediately the dark car lunged up the adjoining on-ramp and was only a few cars lengths behind.

Round one was a draw.

It occurred to me as we passed City Avenue that my pursuer probably didn't know where I was going. He might have thought I was bound for the Hall or at least Center City. I made him worry by taking a path that offered a second choice, over the Twin Bridges and up the Roosevelt Expressway. I was directing half attention forward, half back, as I put on my right blinker as if taking the downtown route.

He was waiting for me to make my move. I floored it and dodged in front of my 18-wheel blocking-back, earning more honking. Cars were zipping left and right like tadpoles in a pond as traffic streamed in from the City Avenue on-ramp and went left or right. At the last moment, hopefully screened by the truck, I cut left, kicking up debris in the narrow shoulder of the highway split.

I heard a screech and a thunk and saw briefly in the rearview a bumper ballet complete with pirouettes. I lost the scene around a curve and got off the first chance I got, just in case the dark car managed to get on my tail again.

I stopped along a street in a struggling industrial area, cursing my own behavior and that of whoever goaded me into it, but the thing I really regretted at that moment was that I hadn't gotten into the auto body business.

Chapter Seventeen

By the time I pulled up near Broad and Allegheny, an intersection bustling with doctors, staff and patients from the Temple Hospital and Medical campus as well as a spectrum of North Philadelphia folks, I had put my frankly inexcusable behavior out of my mind. I prowled for a parking spot and regretted that I didn't have a station car. TV trucks splashed with logos ended up on the sidewalk, the median and even in front of hydrants in brazen displays of the fuck-it-we're-the-media attitude that endeared us to all. I ended up a couple of blocks away at a meter.

Councilwoman Doros' office was on the second floor of a building above what in the heart of the barrio would have been a bodega, but here was just a quickie mart offering home-made hoagies and brewery-made beer. The irony factor was very high since beer takeout joints were nuisances all across town. This one was on good behavior because of the nag upstairs but still you could grab a quart of Colt in a paper sleeve that fooled no one and get sloppy on the subway within moments.

I ran into a couple of TV photogs on the way in and was briefly grateful that my radio gear wasn't nearly as bulky as a camera, tripod and often some bored reporter that they're dragging up long flights of stairs. That's why they had to park that close. We were ushered into a back office that in the dim past had been a bedroom. It had a desk, a row of folding chairs and a nice view of an alley, which probably really got hopping after sundown with a forecast of liquor, drugs and machismo with a 40 percent chance of bloodshed coming out of the northwest.

We sat around shooting the shit until a quorum was present (that is, the number one TV and radio stations) at which point Doros entered gracefully and perched behind the desk with its picket fence of microphones.

"Thank you all for coming," she began. "I have acquired some information that alternately causes my blood to boil and freeze. The arson squad had told me that the warehouse fire the other night, inside my councilmanic district..."

Uh-oh, I thought, here we go.

"Was in a building owned by my "old friends" the Rosen-Philadelphia Real Estate Investment Trust and so vastly over-insured that the REIT is now a target of the arson probe. Some of you, Frank, Lenny, " as she pointed to a couple community newspaper guys, "know how I have been struggling with these people for years, but this, this, is simply intolerable. I am prepared to introduce legislation requiring City oversight of REITs, their projects and their books." For a moment as she took a long slow breath, the only sound in the room was frantic scribbling. Even I realized this was major. Such City intrusion in private concerns was unheard-of. Crippling taxation and red tape, sure, but actually cracking open the finances would be like Atlanta ordering Coke to reveal the secret formula.

"I have copies here of draft legislation I'll be introducing, and a document laying out the investors in this scheme. One, " and she zeroes in on me, "is a major player in the local media, Warren Nash, owner of WPN."

My mind was going all different ways at once. One part was busy taking notes, weighing quotes and noting track numbers on the recorder so I could find them later. Another was running the unlikely political calculus on this bill, that if it were not DOA then private redevelopment was: no company wanted to open its books, especially to City bean counters looking for trouble. A third part of my thoughts were on how the hell was I going to quote my own boss? A fourth one, where the hell did she get this document, which previously had been in the hands of Agent Semyenovic? The final part was in the corner of my head rocking back and forth, alternately drooling and shrieking.

Suddenly, Councilwoman Doros was no longer attractive but the villain in the new flick, Reporter on the Verge of a Nervous Breakdown.

The rest of the news conference passed in a blur and I ended up sitting there for a moment staring at the REIT investors list. My boss, the crook. This was no surprise but now it wasn't just our little secret. I packed up my gear, figuring that I'd give TBC a call once I got outside to apprise him of the situation, and grab a reaction.

I was following one of the cameramen out when I caught a glimpse across the street. Idling in a bus stop zone was a dark car, with a crumpled fender and a taillight dangling by a wire.

I backed up in the entry hall and ran into one of the TV photogs coming down the stairs.

"Whoa, whoa," he said, juggling equipment worth a down payment on a decent house.

"Sorry," I said and ducked through a connecting door into the quickie mart. I went to the counter. "You got a fire exit?" The clerk twitched a thumb but didn't look up from his girly magazine. This, evidently, was not the first time he'd gotten the request.

I threaded through the displays, ducked behind the beer cooler and there it was, not even closed. A moment later I was in the alley, stepping over a man asleep under a blanket in the lee of a dumpster. Trash was his pillow. Because Semyenovic or whoever was in the dark car could see up and down Allegheny, I turned left and headed south to the next cross street. I figured I had maybe five more minutes before my shadow realized that I had used the back door.

I crossed Broad in a crowd of people, trying to hide among them without appearing to. I walked east on Clearfield with growing confidence that I'd shaken my tail but growing worry about the FBI, the REIT and the fire. As I approached my car, I was not planning to file from the scene, just get the heck out of there, but two men emerged from a boxy gray car across the street that might as well have had "police undercover unit" spray painted on its side and I stopped stunned.

It was Pell and Dellacourt.

"Hey," Captain Pell waved, "got a minute?"

Maybe in this neighborhood the first instinct was to run from the police but that's if you have somewhere to go and something to hide. I didn't think I had either.

So I guess I was doubly surprised that as soon as he got within arm's length, Pell smacked me upside the head and pushed me onto the hood of the nearest vehicle. Dellacourt slapped handcuffs on me and they hauled me across to their car.

"What's this all about?" I yelled.

"Quiet," Pell ordered. "Get in." They helped me, with exaggerated caution and a hand on my head to keep it from bumping the doorframe, into the back. They both got in the front. "Welcome to my office," said Pell, turning in the passenger's seat. "What's with you and the FBI?"

"How do you know about that? How did you find me?"

"Be grateful I did. That is one pissed-off agent, Smitkovich or something."

"Semyenovic."

"Yeah, the Highway Patrol boys got your name from him at some accident scene out on the Expressway. You know anything about that?"

"I drove here on the Expressway but didn't see any accident."

"Uh-huh. Well then, lucky thing that Agent Semyenovic is the only one giving you up as the cause. Everyone else says it was him."

"Anyone hurt?"

"Why? Got a guilty conscience?"

"I'm a people person. It's my one fault. What do you want, anyway? And would you mind letting me loose?"

"In due time. My friend on the Arson Squad wanted me to ask you some more questions about that REIT. He's gotten zip out of the Feds."

"Well, you're in luck. Councilwoman Doros just put the whole thing in the headlines. You'll find a copy of the REIT's investors list in my bag. Go ahead and grab it." It took some squirming since my bag was trapped by my handcuffed arms, but Pell snagged the papers and gave them a quick scan.

"Thanks. This will help him out, but won't it get you in trouble with the boss?"

"It'll be a challenge crafting this story and keeping my job. I already punched out his nephew."

"Good for you," Pell shoved the papers into a coat pocket. "What do you know about the warehouse fire?"

"Nothing but what I reported and have now turned over to you. It appears TBC, Mr. Nash, stands to make a pretty penny from the fire but so do all the other investors in the REIT. Are you guys having any luck with who set it?"

"Not that I know of. Whoever it was slipped past some pretty good alarm systems to do it." I nodded. In that section of town, they put chains on trashcans.

"Listen," said Pell. "I'm going to need your help with something tomorrow."

Color me surprised. "My help?"

"Yeah, can you arrange to come down to the Roundhouse," police headquarters, "some time, maybe 11 or noon? It's some loose ends in your brother-in-law's case."

"What sort of loose ends?"

"The loose kind."

"Sure, fine. Just don't give me any shit if I report on it."

"I wouldn't worry a bit. Just come to the main entrance and have them page me."

Pell got out of the car and helped me back to the sidewalk. Dellacourt freed me from the cuffs. "How did you find me? You put a tracking device on my car?" I asked.

"I wish I had that kind of budget. Nah, I'd put out an alert on your license plate, watch and report, and the Highway Patrol guys alerted the District here when your number came up."

"Wait a minute." I was rubbing my wrists to restore some circulation. "They knew I was coming here?"

"Agent What's-his-name said so. Like a good baseball double-play, Highway Patrol to street cop to me." Pell flat-handed me on the back. "Stay into trouble."

"Isn't that supposed to be stay out of trouble?"

He shrugged. "Christmas was last month. We're out of miracles now."

I got in my car without even bothering to stow the gear in the trunk and took a zigzag course through one-way streets that almost got me lost. Eventually, I was back on the Roosevelt Extension, past the split where the accident happened and heading for the station without further incident, for once.

Carrie looked up as I entered the newsroom. "You're not going to believe this," I said. "Councilwoman Doros has put out a list of investors in the warehouse that burned on Monday. It includes TBC and she's gone public with all this dirty laundry that makes it look as if they might have done it for the insurance."

"Well?" She swiveled in her chair and leaned back.

"Well, sure, they might, but right now there's exactly zero evidence that they did. Anyway, I have to tell TBC and get his reaction, if any."

"He won't talk."

"Oh, he'll talk. We just won't be able to put it on the radio."

I walked straight to Nash's office, bypassing the new receptionist who appeared to be a temp from Bimbos-R-Us. She smacked on gum while giving fingernails done in black and gray swirls a coat of sealant. But if she could answer the phone or even find the word "attorneys" in the Yellow Pages that would be an improvement.

I knocked on the doorframe and Nash looked up from some papers. "Bernie, what gives?" He gestured me in and I shut the door behind me.

"Remember that stuff from my deposition, about the REIT and the insurance on that warehouse? Well, it's out there now. Councilwoman Doros just made it public."

"Her," was all he said at first. Then he shook his head wearily and went on. "It was bound to happen. I just got off the phone with the insurance company. They're not going to pay a dime until they investigate."

"Do you have any reaction I can put in the story?"

"My reaction is, don't do a story at all."

"I have to."

"Why?"

"It's news."

Nash clutched his hands in front of him. "Why is it news, because a councilwoman with a permanent stick up her ass about REITs and redevelopment calls a news conference? Because it involves me, however tangentially?"

"Gee, I don't know, boss, maybe because of the arson."

"What was it you said to the reporters last night on TV, let the D.A. do his job? How about letting the Arson Squad do its work. I had nothing whatsoever to do with the fire."

"We can't not do this story. It would look as if we're unwilling to cover you."

"So? Even if you feel you have to report on everything negative that someone else says, where's the context? Are you going to be able to, in 45 seconds, not only quote Councilwoman Doros but remind listeners of her longstanding grudge against the very people the Mayor depends on to bring private capital to the inner city? How can her allegation do anything but churn already murky waters? Would you repeat absolutely anyone's allegation about me, like from the guy at the pizza place down the road, whether it has even a snowball's chance of being true, just because it might look like I squelched the story if you don't? That's not reporting. That's like reverse PR, where you only say negative things."

"Look, everyone else...."

He held up a hand. "You don't have to tell me what a monkey-see, monkey-do business news is. We follow the papers, they follow us. TV newsrooms have wall to wall televisions so they can watch every show at once and not miss a chance to follow the leader."

"So you're telling me not to do this?"

"No, I'm not. I haven't interfered editorially yet and I won't now. Maybe you can find a way to cover all the bases in 45 seconds. For the record, no comment."

"That's it?"

"No comment due to the ongoing investigation."

"I get the picture." I left hoping I wasn't radiating the frustration that I felt. If I were a microwave oven, I could have cooked a turkey in a minute flat. He had made some valid points. Doros did have an axe to grind and the provenance of those papers is highly suspect. I was beginning to think she had a friend in the Bureau.

Carrie was no help on the ethical, factual and employment tangle that this story represented. The auction on a collector's edition china plate featuring Weird Al Yankovic was about to end. I sat at the computer, cyber-doodling as I tried to find a way to satisfy everyone's interests and finally just began typing. What I ended up with was this:

A Philadelphia City Councilwoman wants government oversight of Real Estate Investment Trusts. We're Philly's News reporter Bernie Gaston has more:

Councilwoman Elizabeth Doros, a longtime critic of REITs as destroyers rather than redevelopers, wants City Hall to know exactly how they operate....

" I am prepared to introduce legislation requiring city oversight of REITs, their projects and their books."

Doros links her plan to this week's multi-alarm warehouse fire in Kensington. She distributed documents showing that the building was owned by a REIT in which the owner of this station is an investor. He declined comment due to the on-going investigation, but Councilwoman Doros also alleged that the building was over-insured.

At that point I realized I needed another quote and punched in the number for the Mayor's spokesman Thomas Canfield. Pell was wrong about there being no more miracles because Canfield picked up on two rings.

"Tom. Bernie Gaston from WPN. I don't know if you have heard of Councilwoman Doros'..."

"Yes, yes," he interrupted. "Here's our reaction and no tape: The Mayor believes the proposal is unwise and probably unconstitutional. Whether any particular REIT or its investors has done anything illegal will be determined by investigating authorities, but the City oversight of private firms for any purpose other than legitimate investigation would be disastrous. Got that?"

"Ouch," I said.

"Off the record, it's good thing she made this announcement outside City Hall. I have never seen the Mayor this irritated by something that's just political grandstanding. Even the suggestion of this could scare off millions of dollars in investment."

"If you or he want to go on the record, we'll listen."

"We'll see, Bernie. This should be nothing more than a one news cycle wonder. By tomorrow, we will have all moved on."

"Thanks, Tom. See you."

As I hung up, the final lines of the story almost materialized on the screen.

Take Two, A Smart-ass Mystery

	Through a spokesman, the Mayor calls the oversight
proposal "unwise and probably unconstitutional".
	Bernie Gaston, WPN News

	I filed just one version. I don't even know if it aired.

Chapter Eighteen

Jen wasn't nearly as enthused by my handling of the computer problem as I hoped. I didn't expect to be hailed as the conquering hero, although I wouldn't have refused any laurels, but I found her in a deep funk.

Betty had the kids out for a walk when I got home and just getting them into boots, snowsuits and mittens was an exhausting process so Jen lay 3/4 reclined on the couch with the TV news spotlighting some New Jersey high school's canned food drive for MLK Day. After kissing her cheek, I sat down in the narrow space available.

"I went to see Jan today." I might have expected her to elaborate but what else was there to say? I had never been to the women's prison but I had been inside the men's for a story or two. It was all metal and locks and dehumanizing sameness by design. It was not just the lack of a golf course that made prison different from a country club.

"She looked so small and frightened," Jen went on again finally. "She asked about the kids and we cried. She asked about Mom and we cried. She even asked about you. That really made us cry." Jen smiled crookedly to show she was kidding.

I told her about the call from Larry Tierney and she just nodded, but when I suggested we send some flowers she shook her head. "What's the point, BG? They don't like us. They're not going to like us."

"You must have arrangements at the store. No one else has been buying."

"No, they haven't but I think we're in a place where floral arrangements just don't matter any more." What a strange attitude for a florist, I marveled, when the usual approach was to pedal the petals no matter what. Say it with roses and see how it goeses.

Betty and the brood returned shortly. She was a little hoarse from trying to keep them from flinging themselves into traffic but all four kids had such rosy cheeks they looked as if Hummel figurines had come to life. I helped extricate them from their winter gear and then get a serious round of dolls going.

Betty and Jen had dinner pretty much done but I helped by setting the table and filling an assortment of Sippy cups with milk. Samantha and Elizabeth might protest being treated like babies but they were just as spill-prone as the younger two. The meal of pork chops, Brussels sprouts and rice went down easily among the grown-ups although the kids poked those little cabbages around on their plates as if to tease them to death. They each had to eat at least one and Lorraine chewed hers as if we had substituted lug nuts in acid.

Frankie started fussing soon after dinner and was circling the drain by 7:30. Not raised in our hard way/easy way methodology, he insisted on both and was crying and thumping on the closed door to the bedroom even after a story.

"We need his crib or playpen, probably his high chair, too," Jen sighed and I knew what that meant, road trip, but I was surprised that Betty volunteered to go too. She pulled boots on over thermal socks and we suited up for battle with the cold. We left Jen cuddling the three girls in front of the TV. The tantrum upstairs had already faded.

The drive to the Tierneys was certainly a lot easier than during the storm. Betty asked about my day and I gave her the Reader's Digest version, leaving out my exploits on the Expressway. Since I was behind the wheel, I didn't want her to worry that I could be as bad a driver as I had been.

The Tierney's street seemed so empty. The TV trucks and their stage lights were long gone, along with the various official vehicles. A few shards of yellow police tape clung to tree trunks, and the snow, so fluffy during the storm, was under a crunchy sheen of ice compacted by the midday sun.

I saw that the driveway and walk both needed clearing. Frank usually did that, I thought, so I parked in the street and helped Betty up the lawn in the footprints from the other night. We let ourselves in and then without a word stood staring at the red shadow in the rug.

"Oh, my," Betty said after a moment. Maybe, until that instant, she had somehow not believed that her daughter had killed a man. The bloodstain was a little hard to ignore.

"I'm going to get some salt to throw on the driveway and walk," I said and looked in the coat closet which, drat the luck, had only coats and boots. Betty turned into the family room and began to collapse the playpen, as I walked through the house, retracing my steps with Pell how many hours ago. Forty-five, forty-six?

I flipped on the back yard light and then the wall switch in the garage. It smelled funny in there, musty and old, but I found a snow shovel with a decent edge on it and some snowmelt compound in a bag and hauled them back the way I'd come in. In passing, I grabbed the high chair from the kitchen. It made for full arms but one less trip.

After stowing the highchair in the back seat of the Honda, I started with the front stoop, chiseling away the worst of the ice, which had already claimed Jen as a victim. A couple good whacks were all it took, then a noisy scrape and a handful of salt. The walk had a few rough spots with shoe-shaped ice clods but I was popping them off often intact with a shove of the shovel.

It was about the time I began to tackle the driveway that I heard a crunch and looked up to see a man in a winter coat, light pants and slippers approaching across the frozen lawn.

"Hey," I said conversationally, leaning on the shovel handle.

"Hey," he responded. "I'm Brad Sellers from two doors down."

"Bernie Gaston, Frank and Jen's brother-in-law."

"Yeah, listen, I'm shocked about what happened and what I have to say is such small potatoes, but when I heard noise over here I decided, what the heck." He paused for a response but since I'd never laid eyes on the guy before I figured the ball was in his court. "Uh, the other night there was a car blocking the alley. I had to back out onto Granger Rd. in the storm. Pretty dangerous."

I had no idea what this guy was talking about but to avoid prolonging the pointless conversation I surrendered right away.

"I'm sorry for your inconvenience. We'll make sure it doesn't happen again." Which shouldn't be hard, I figured, since I didn't have anything to do with it happening the first time.

"Well, thanks." Brad seemed to expect there would be something else but I ended our heart-to-heart by resuming my noisy scraping. He went home to TV and a bottle of gin, no doubt.

It took me a good half hour to do the driveway and the length of sidewalk along the street. A few cars passed by, splashing a mixture of road-salt, gravel and slush onto mine. Car washes did a booming business the weekend after a storm.

I heard a mechanical whine from inside the house as I opened the front door. Betty was using a rug-scrubber on the bloodstain, which had a foamy beard in spots where she hadn't slurped it up. From the looks of things, Frank was clinging to the carpet more than he had clung to life.

"Betty!" I yelled to pierce the din. She startled and looked over at me, then turned off the racket.   "Out, out, damned spot," I said, exhausting my knowledge of Shakespeare in one phrase.   "That'll never come out. We'll have to replace the carpet, maybe even the subflooring."

"I had to do something," she said meekly and I understood all too well. Despite the futility, she finished up while I returned the winter weapons to the garage. I turned out the backyard lights and made sure the door was latched and locked. Betty had her coat on again and the playpen in hand. I offered to carry it but she said, "Frankie's my boy now."

We secured the front door and followed the newly cleared walk and driveway out to the car. I used the remote to beep the trunk open and Betty was about to heave the playpen into it when a car engine roared down the street. I could see the vehicle, a dark sedan with high beams on, racing toward us, nearly blinding us as it closed in.

"Betty, get back," I said and pushed her and the playpen onto the lawn where they went down in a heap. The car raced past near enough to take the chrome off my driver's side wing mirror, hitting a rich vein of salt melt which fountained all over me. The car vanished down the street with barely a blink of brake lights.

Dripping and dirty, I turned to help Betty up.

"What an asshole," she said.

Chapter Nineteen:
Friday

I was having some sort of anxiety dream (do you think?) when the phone began ringing and I swam back to semi-consciousness. As I stumbled across the bedroom to grab it, I noticed Jen had not budged. Her father was long dead, her mother was on the couch downstairs, her kids were asleep, her sister was in jail and her brother-in-law was in the morgue so there really wasn't much worth getting up for at that hour.

"Hello," I managed to rasp.

"Bernie, this is Warren. I need you to get over here."

Okay, there are certain calls you never expect to get. "Hello, Mr. Gaston, the President is holding on line one," would be an example. "Sweetie, this is Jen. Go watch a movie. Your honey-do list can wait" would be another. I pulled the handset back from my head and looked at it, as if it could somehow explain the outflowing foolishness.

"Huh?" I responded, still trying to load a language upgrade into my computer of a brain. "Warren who?"

"Warren Nash, for God's sake! Look, I have a situation here and I'd rather not discuss it on the phone. I need you to come over."

"Now?" I looked at the clock. 2:30 a.m.

"Yes, now! Something has happened and it involves you too, I dare say."

"You're at the station?"

"No, my house. Are you always this dense? You ought to get more sleep."   There was a moment of silence while I struggled not to tell him to fuck off truly, but I remembered I needed the job.

"Give me the address...."

I sneaked a quick shower and shave before dressing and pecking Jen's cheek. She still didn't budge and looked so peaceful hogging all the covers that I wanted to plunge right back in. But duty called.

I made a quick check of the kids, now distributed between the two other bedrooms (Frankie doing a headstand in his crib), grabbed my coat, keys and whatnot before slipping into the night. My car, of course, was as cold as a freezer and I sat there cooling my heels while warming the engine. The needle had barely budged when I crunched over ice in backing out of the parking space.

Warren Peter Nash lived on the other side of the world from Benfranklin, on Philly's fabled Main Line. He was currently a bachelor, puttering around a mansion that hiring a firm of shark lawyers had allowed him to keep out of the hands of the first Mrs. The other two had pre-nups and had to settle for some lovely parting gifts and a check with far-fewer zeroes than they might have liked.

Getting to Merion required going end to end on the Boulevard, all but deserted at this hour. I couldn't help but note the decrescendo of rowhouses and twins lining it. In the Far Northeast, they were spotless, their walks shoveled, their windows aglow from within. By Oxford Circle, most were still looking good but it was more of a struggle, with older homes sagging in shadow, caught in the urban undertow of decay. By the time I crossed Front Street the housing stock was heading for bankruptcy and off to the right in Logan was this big empty space, crisscrossed only by streetlamps, where an entire neighborhood had been removed. This wasn't the place that burned to the ground when a Mayor ordered a bomb dropped in a confrontation with some radicals. This one died not by fire but water, bulldozed because it had begun to sink inexorably into the creek bed over which it had been poorly built at the end of the 19th century.

The 12-lane part of the Boulevard drains into the Boulevard Extension the way a sleepy mountain lake births whitewater rapids. I kicked the speed up to 65 as stoplights fell away behind me. The Extension expressway carried me under the Broad St. Subway and over the railroad, past an imposing hillside that holds back a billion gallons in a city reservoir and past the place where I sat only yesterday to decompress from my Mad Max impression. Once across the southbound Twin Bridge, it was about a quarter mile on the Schuylkill Expressway, off at City Avenue and up the hill looking for Montgomery Avenue.

In the City, important streets have lots of lights. They blaze almost like day. In Merion, darkness is chic, and there aren't that many muggers, so I navigated down a suburban road, squinting at street signs about the size of candy bars which PennDOT and townships alike usually located behind tree limbs. I missed my turn twice before, by process of elimination, I turned onto a street that, if possible, was darker, narrower and richer. The houses were no longer even visible, lost in the night behind high walls and long snowy lawns at the end of gated drives.

Address numbers were hard to come by, so I drove leaning over the steering wheel as if being six inches closer would make them bloom in the darkness.

It might have been quarter of four before I found the place and pulled up to the speaker by the gate. I pushed its button and didn't have to wait long.

"About damn time," said Nash's tinny voice, which battled the noise of a motor pulling the gate aside. I drove up a narrow crescent of cobblestones to the front of a home

I can only describe as "whoa." It rested under skeletal trees, a stone-fronted edifice that probably was to the money pit what a quarry is to a snake hole. It loomed in the gloom as I got out of my car and wondered if I'd have to use the servant's entrance, but the front door, a massive thing of brass-clasped wood opened with a squeal of hinges. There stood Nash, wrapped in a smoking jacket that was at least two decades out of date. He carried a flashlight and made a show of trying to illuminate the steps for me, although a fluttering Tinkerbelle would have been more help.

"Come, come," he said, ushering me in with an arm over my shoulder. With a clunk, the door closed and I looked around at a two-story foyer with twin curving staircases on left and right. Without pleasantries, I followed him through a door and suddenly I was in his museum to deforestation. This place had dark wood floors, walls and ceilings, with crown molding and chair rail molding along with the regular floorboard stuff. He had artwork in gilded frames every few feet. Despite his urgings to move forward, my eye caught one and I stopped.

"I studied this in art history," I said.

"Yes, yes, it's a Matisse," he interrupted testily. "He painted two. I gave one to the museum." He dragged me further into his lair. The next room we passed, despite its cave-like lighting, seemed to reach out a grab me. I stopped suddenly and his forward momentum peeled his arm off me.

There was a car in the room. "Is that..." I began.

He sighed, although without much conviction, and said, "Lights, display." The room somehow heard and obeyed. Illumination rose up slowly and incompletely to reveal, not more wood, but what appeared to be the inside of a cavern, complete with stalactites, stalagmites and glistening multicolored spots that looked as if subterranean water flowed. But in the center of the room, framed by a spotlight that wasn't really trying, stood a Batmobile.

I turned to Nash, stunned. A Matisse and a Batmobile? How much money did this guy have? What other treasures were squirreled away around in here? Why wasn't I being paid more?

"Come, come," he said, dragging me by the arm deeper into the mansion. I've been to the Philadelphia Museum of Art a few times. You entered a gallery or walked down a hallway and it was masterpiece, another masterpiece, another another masterpiece, ho hum a masterpiece, oh would you cut it out with the masterpieces already? That was what his house was like.

Eventually we reached a back room, his office by the look of it, with a massive desk that could have been used as an aircraft carrier deck dominating a sea of Persian carpet. I was taking it all in, so far past intimidated that I think I wanted my blankie, when he stopped to face me.

"Some one broke in here tonight."

"You were burglarized? Don't you have an alarm system?" I was scanning the room and the row after row of framed photos and awards that popped like glass mushrooms from the brown loam of the paneling.

"Of course I do. It's top of the line and this guy went through it like I'd left all the doors wide open."

"What'd he take?"

"Not just take," he responded mysteriously. "That picture was smashed by the intruder. Go take a look." I strode over to a now-empty frame grinning with jagged glass teeth. I knelt by the debris on the floor and, chastened by TV forensics shows, pushed a crumbled certificate and photograph around with the point of my pen.

"No need to do that," Nash said, and reached over my shoulder to grab the two sheets. He smoothed them out on the edge of his desk and handed them to me. So much for my CSI career. I took them.

One was a certificate of appreciation from Philadelphia City Council, passed by a voice vote and duly signed by the Council President. It thanked WPN for community service preceding some flooding just downstream from the station in the Manayunk neighborhood. We had gone beyond putting word of the expected high water on the radio, and slapped a loudspeaker on a station van to make the rounds through streets in the flood plain. People took preparations and damage was minimal. Since I had been driving the van, I was alongside Nash and the assorted Council members in the photo.

"Hmmph," I offered noncommittally.

"Come," said Nash, who guided me by the arm to the other side of the USS Desk. A lower drawer equipped with a lock had been forced open, judging by the pry marks. There were some papers inside but otherwise it was unremarkable. I aimed a quizzical look at Nash.

"I had a gun in there, a revolver."

"He took the gun but left the paintings, and the Batmobile." The master of the obvious, that's me.

"He left something else, too." Again with the arm grab. If I were female, I'd have had him for harassment and then I'd own the Matisse. My home simply didn't have the floor space for a Batmobile.

We went back out into the main hall and turned down another, clumping along past more framed wonders until we ducked through a metal door into a garage big enough to host the Auto Show. There were six cars ranging from really expensive to don't ask, but he directed my attention to a red plastic gas can in the corner. We walked over.

"A present from our intruder."

"You don't own a gas can?"

"I don't mow my lawn. You see any garden tools in here? That's why God made Mexicans." Now he unfurled a handkerchief from his pocket and unscrewed the cap on the gas can's long neck. From the way he hoisted it, the can was empty. "Sniff."

I did. It was gas, all right, but different.

"Diesel fuel..." He let the revelation hang.

"How..." I wondered.

"I run a trucking company, too, remember. As to how it got here, come. Let me show you. "

He directed me back into the house. "Our visitor bypassed the alarm like a pro but he didn't count on my separate surveillance system. It's state of the art, wireless, with cameras about the size of quarters. There's one," he pointed but all I saw in the direction of his gesture was a doorframe.

We re-entered his office and he swung aside two doors revealing a sparkling new HDTV and some video equipment nestled in a built-in cabinet. Nash grabbed a remote, fired up the monitor and then stooped to actually press a button on a DVR.. The screen flared to life, divided into six sectors, but each was large enough to be fairly detailed even if in black and white. One subscreen showed the room in which we were standing.

"Watch." The playback must have been cued because right away a figure in a trench coat and a balaclava entered the room almost casually. He scanned left and right with a professional's practiced gaze before plunking himself at the desk. His gloved hands opened the unlocked drawers in a flash. He jiggled the locked once before a six-inch pry bar he pulled from his belt made short work of popping it open as well. There went the revolver, out of the drawer and into his coat pocket with a quick movement, and in went a piece of paper. He sprang to his feet and was heading around the desk when something caught his eye. He leaned in, peering at a picture on the wall, then pulled back a fist and punched it square-on.

The intruder then shook his hand, as if glass or perhaps common sense had penetrated the glove, but then he used the pry bar to flick the contents out of the frame. He crushed the picture and the commendation and left.

Nash stopped the playback.

"You saw him stick something in the drawer?" Nash asked. I nodded. He dug into his pants pocket and came out with a folded sheet of paper, which he twitched in my direction. I took and unfolded it.

It was the investors list from the REIT, although not exactly as I remembered it. There were fewer names on it, and mine was one of them. My mind was whirling with the permutations of just how exactly not good this was.

We had gone from dogged FBI agent pursuing my crook of a boss to whacked-out, way off the deep end FBI agent trying to catch us both in a frame-up.

"So," Nash interrupted my thoughts after a moment, "I assume you have figured the guy on the video to be Agent Semyenovic. What's his game?"

"He was a little over the top at the my deposition. I didn't think much of it until Wednesday night. I was at the D.A.'s office on my sister-in-law's case and he was waiting, no, make that lurking, in the shadows. He seemed, I don't know, brittle, frazzled. He said the case was ready to crack but I think he was talking about himself."

"This is really beginning to piss me off," Nash said, smacking a fist into a palm. "I'd call my lawyer right this instant if he wasn't in Vail doing the horizontal tango with that paralegal of his."

"We could call the cops," I ventured.

"Oh, yes, that's just great. Let's invite them into the frame-up. We can be fitted for matching handcuffs."

The phone on his desk chirped. "Who?" he wondered and grabbed the handset. "Yes? Uh-huh. No, I didn't. Look, look, I'll be right out."

He hung up and responded to my puzzled look. "That's the intercom at the front gate. The police are already here."

Chapter Twenty

Nash signaled for me to follow him back the way we had come in, clumping down the front steps and the driveway to the re-closed front gate. Two uniformed police officers cooled their heels outside, back-lit by the headlights of their patrol car. They swung heavy flashlights, also good for noggin knockin', in our direction.

"Officers, " Nash began, "what brings you out at this time of night?" It was meant to be an icebreaker but you'd have needed Coast Guard cutter with these two.

"We got a call of a burglary in progress here, sir. We came to check it out," said the taller officer who wore corporal's stripes.

Nash risked a quick glance at me before responding. "There has been no burglary. I'm Warren Nash, the homeowner here. This is my associate, Bernie Gaston." The word "associate" called up unwelcome wise guy images in my mind, like I was now a made member of the WPN gang.

"May I see some ID, sir?" Phrased as a question, it was not one, so I pried my driver's license out of my wallet. Nash put mine together with his and handed them through the gate to the Corporal. Lerner, I think his nametag said.

The other cop, Pinciotti, kept his torch on both of us, watching for any suspicious behavior.

"Very good, sir," said Lerner, handing the laminated cards back through the slats. "Perhaps we should have a look around anyway."

"I don't think that will be necessary," Nash said. "How did all this nonsense get started?"

"We got an anonymous 911 call."

"Probably a prank."

"The caller said something about evidence to be found. The call quality was not very good."

"Nor was the information. A non-existent burglary means non-existent evidence."

"The perp could still be on the property," Lerner suggested.

"I have burglar alarms up the yin-yang here, officer. You have no reports from my security company, do you?"

"No, sir."

"Then, let's write it off as a prank. Maybe you can trace the caller's phone number and suggest that he stop wasting your time."

"Yes, sir," said Lerner although he didn't sound convinced. "Good night, sir." He and Pinciotti got back in their cruiser. We could hear the squawk of the radio as they pulled away in the darkness.

Nash stood still until they had gone out of sight. "That prick Semyenovic thinks he's yanking my chain. I've been yanked by pros, not some bipolar wanker. He probably thought I'd get all stupid when I saw his handiwork and call the cops myself. Fat chance. So he gets impatient when I don't and calls it in himself." Nash paused, making a mental calculation.

"We have to go on the offensive," he said after a moment. "I'll get that lazy ass lawyer of mine out of the sack and have him file a writ or a shit or a tit to get us some breathing room from Agent Orange there. Let's get his bosses on his ass. Once the papers are filed, we'll put it on the air. Christ, I own a radio station. I know I'll have at least one reporter at my news conference." He elbowed me conspiratorially.

"You know, we might actually need the police," I suggested. "Not these suburban guys, but the city cops. That gas can is evidence. Obviously, he's trying to frame you for the fire but that cuts both ways. You didn't touch the can, did you?"

He gave me a pained expression. "Of course not, but I don't want them out here. I'll have some people check the place for prints." He saw my look, shrugged. "Hey, crime scene techs moonlight. I know some people who know some people."

I bet you do, I thought.

"He has your gun," I reminded Nash. "We could be in danger."

"If he wanted to shoot me, he already had a gun. No, he wants to shoot someone else and frame me. "

"Then report the gun as stolen. Tell the cops you hadn't noticed it at first but you discovered it missing later on."

"If someone is shot with it, it'd just look like I was trying to establish an alibi in advance." He clapped me on the shoulder, decision taken, then snagged a twenty from his wallet. "Burglaries always make me hungry. Go get us some chow. There's a 24 hour diner on City Line. I'll take a Denver omelet and sausage. Get yourself whatever. I have some calls to make."

"Boss," I said as casually as I could, "when did you discover the break-in? Were you home?"

'Nah," he replied barely breaking stride, "I was out test-driving the next ex-Mrs. Nash. Lots of junk in the trunk, good front bumpers, and low mileage." He scooted back into the house, leaving me a glorified go-fer. Come to think of it, maybe not even all that glorified.

Hey, at least he was buying.

The gates opened automatically from the inside as I guided my car toward them. On this residential street, at this hour, there was no traffic, but on Montgomery there were the headlights of the early risers, the first drops in the morning commuter wave. I station-hopped, barely listening to the headlines, which went in one ear and out the other.

It wasn't far to the diner and it was actually pretty busy, given the hour. I found a parking spot, walked inside and settled at the counter while looking at the menu. I didn't really feel like eating, even though my stomach was telling me how lonely it was. This situation was spiraling out of control and I could see no good place to be. By myself, I was a sitting duck, or a dead one. Cozying up to TBC provided some safety in numbers and the thought that he was a higher profile catch, although if it came to being the better target, maybe I was on point in this patrol.

I placed the take-out order and passed the time by perusing the Inquirer's front page and Metro section. An update on Frank's murder had a few details that I didn't know, like an explanation of a computer-enhancing technique they were using to work with the snowy footprints in the Tierney backyard. Pell had said something like that, but why they needed such attention, I didn't know.

The food arrived steaming in its bagged Styrofoam containers. I paid, pocketed the receipt and change and dodged an arriving couple to butt the door open. A gangly Goth teen was coming up the three steps from the parking lot and he reached past my shoulder to keep the door from closing.

He didn't make it. His outstretched arm, clad in a sleeve of a dark blue wool coat, slammed into my face, knocking me into the railing, as the echo of thunder rolled over me. My legs gave way and I tumbled under the railing down on the other side of the steps. The breakfast bag plopped into the snow next to me, sideways and leaking. Breath knocked out of me, I was dimly aware of a second shot that pinged off the siding and of people screaming and running around in reaction.

The teen was moaning and gripping his arm, which was now leaking red. A couple of brave people from inside crawled toward him and dragged him through the doorway. I angled up against the steps, peering over them in the direction of the shots. I couldn't see anything. There might have been a puff of gun smoke out toward City Avenue but in this light who could tell?

When 15 seconds passed without any further fusillade, I pushed the take-out as together as best I could and scooted toward my car, keeping low. I zapped the lock with the remote and then fumbled with the keys while hunkered down with my head almost in the passenger seat. With my right hand shaking, the key finally found purchase and the engine started. I heard sirens in the distance as I pulled out on City Avenue and, slowly, slowly, everybody act natural, drove back to stately Nash manor.

There seemed to me to be several choices here: someone was shooting at Goth boy, someone was shooting at the diner or someone was shooting at me. I'd have wagered dollars to donuts that those bullets were going to trace right back to Nash's gun. No surprise, but I discovered I didn't like the feeling of cross-hairs on my back.

Nash beeped me through the gate and as I parked I noticed that breakfast had made a fast break, leaking all over my car. Thank God for removable floor mats.

I scooped up the soggy sack, hands on the bottom to prevent any more mess. "Got a paper towel?" I asked Nash at the door.

"What the hell happened?"

"I think we found your gun."

He hustled me into the kitchen where we wiped down the breakfast containers and put what was still edible on plates. Nash had made coffee, a previously unsuspected talent, and he thunked a mug down in front of me at a bistro table. Maybe I should have asked for a Diet Coke.

"Tell me what happened." I did, and he took advantage of my talking to get way ahead of me eating.

"If it was your gun, you should have told the cops," I finished.

Through a mouthful of food he replied, "Doesn't matter. It wasn't registered anyway."

My turn to choke. "You think you might have mentioned that before?"

"Need to know."

I glanced at a clock. 6:15, and I wondered if I could put any of this on my timesheet.

Nash finished eating and stuffed the foam container into a trash compactor. I felt some pressure to finish up, so I wasn't far behind him.

"Why don't you call the station and see if they have anything for you to do." Nash said in his "boss" voice. "I'll take another stab at getting that shyster of mine off his ass and on Semyenovic's."

"I'm not sure I should even leave," I protested. I had discovered that being shot at was very unpleasant.

"You want me to call you a cab, or a nanny? Grow up! If he followed you and actually wanted to kill you, how hard would it have been to wait by your car and feed you a lead breakfast?"

"Well, when you put it that way..."

"Or staying here? He's already shown he can break in. By the way, remind me to chew that alarm company a new one. We have to assume he's toying with us, for whatever demented reason he has. I'm hoping that by this afternoon we can get this guy's boss to yank on his leash."

"I think he's already off the leash and out of the yard."

Nash nodded silently, acknowledging that this could be the truth. "All the more reason for you to move your family elsewhere for a few days. Do you have any place to go?"

I thought about it for a moment. Betty's house was too small for the new, giant-size us, but nobody was using the Tierney house for the moment. I could buy a cheap area rug to cover up the bloodstain.

I shrugged. "Maybe. I'll have to discuss it with Jen."

"You see, that's why you're still married and I'm not. I'd have just told the lying bitch, here's what's happening and if you don't like it, walk. Come to think of it, that is what I said, and a couple of them did."

He clapped me on the shoulder and left the kitchen. I slipped my phone off its belt clip and dialed the newsroom. Silcox answered and told me to head down to the Penn campus to do some sidebar material on a wire story about college safety. If there's one thing that's as standard in radio news as following the morning paper, it's interviewing random people who don't know anything about the story but may have an opinion on the issue. It's variously called man-on-the-street, or MOS, vox-pop, which is short for the Latin, vox populi, voice of the people, or AAA, ask any asshole.

"Sure," I said, trying to let my disinterest overflow in my voice. Silcox was, as usual, oblivious.

"Hey, Beanie," he said, just as I was about to disconnect, "that guy called again from the MLK Day group. He's getting kind of antsy that you two keep missing."

"I'll call him later." Like later in my life. Like sometime when I cared. "Bye."

I let myself out and, at the end of the driveway, instead of going right, turned left. Dawn was hinting in the east, peeking between gnarled extrusions of some of the houses. I scanned as I drove, not really sure what I was looking for. Maybe that dark and damaged car. Or a nondescript van, the likes of which FBI agents might use for stakeout, but the residents of this street would sooner die than set foot in. The road wound into another and then a third. I saw nothing but the homes of people who had made better career choices than me. Finally I found City Avenue again and, rather than heading back to the Schuylkill, slid onto Lancaster Avenue, overland into town.

The streets of West Philadelphia were coming alive with children racing commuters for the bus stop, competing for precious cleared sidewalk space. Traffic puttering through, still slow because of lingering ice that reformed each night from yesterday's snow melt. Hit a slicked-up trolley track and you'd do a triple axle that even the snotty French judge would give a 7.9. Fairmount Park lay still and white as I drove past its fringe. It looked as if the city's lungs had frozen, mid-breath, and awaited April to exhale.

I maneuvered down onto the Schuylkill at Girard and slipped off at 30th Street onto a roundabout that cut between the Athenian Temple-like train station and a blue glass-clad skyscraper cut to look like a ship's prow running hard with the wind. There were precious few unmetered on-street parking spaces in this section of town where the University of Pennsylvania and Drexel University lay entwined like lovers on sticky sheets. But I wasn't planning to be there all morning so I grabbed a spot on Walnut Street, paid for the max 2 hours with my SmartCard and began to prowl for spokesvictims.

There's an art to MOS, which I hate as much as I did door-to-door huckstering for fundraisers back in middle school. In summer-time, I would look for a sidewalk or patio cafe where people might have the time to talk. In deep winter, though, it was tougher. Nobody lingered in the cold, so I stood near a Starbucks and approached a few women, mike flag raised, so they didn't think I was the same sort of mad raper-stomper that I was asking them about.

After several minutes of a five to one rejection ratio, I had five or six good comments, all utterly forgettable, but enough to make this sack of shit into, well, at least a more presentable sack of shit. They were the usual mixture of "Campus security should be a priority. You can't learn if you're scared," "I feel safe. There's a cop on every corner around here," and the ever-popular, but not-for-air "This wouldn't be a problem if all men were castrated." It's nice to be appreciated.

I called back to the station and Silcox slotted me in the 7:30 news block. That gave me a few minutes so I found a low wall to lean on and brushed away the snow and ice. Pedestrians moved past me heedlessly in their morning waltz with cars, trucks, buses and the occasional lunatic on a bike or skateboard.

I did my first live-shot, talk, talk, talk, tape, tape, tape, talk, talk. I hoped it made sense because I couldn't have told you what I said even ten seconds later. I was considering whether to spend the next half hour in a coffee shop, warming my insides with a cup o' Joe, when my phone rang.

"Gaston," I said.

"Jen," replied the familiar voice of my wife. "Where'd you get to?"

"You won't believe. TBC called me in the middle of the night. He'd been burglarized, we think by that crazy FBI agent who deposed me the other day." I decided not to tell her about the shooting just then. Maybe later over a glass of wine, or vodka.

"Burgled by the FBI? BG, what is he, the Mayor?"

I sighed, "This is way over my head, Jen, way over. All of a sudden, I'm Nash's new best friend. Do you know, he has a fucking Batmobile in his house, a movie prop set up in its own room dressed up like the Batcave?"

"He's paying you way too little."

"My thoughts exactly." I knew I loved that woman for a reason. "Anyway, I'm at Penn now doing the Starbucks shift."

"Can you be home at 10?"

"Ten? This morning?"

"Yes, 10 a.m. this morning. I just got off the phone with that woman from Children's Services. She's coming by to check up on Samantha and Frankie and I'd like you here." So I was thinking, I'd like to be there too, another chance to see Katrina Colarusso, lusting in my heart on a date chaperoned by my wife. No, no, it was way to much like an Ingmar Bergman movie.

"I'll see what I can do, hon, but since I'm Johnny Paycheck for the time being I'd better keep them happy back at the station. TBC was already calling his lawyer to do something about this FBI yahoo and it's got three-inch headline written all over it."

"But B.G.," she pouted, "I feel so alone. Jan might not be coming home."

"Jen, Jen, you have to get a grip. If anyone can get Jan off the hook it's that Hanratty woman. Crocodiles run from her."

She snorted, about the best display of humor I'd expect under the circumstances. "It's just that I'm scared they'll take the kids. I bet the Tierneys are telling her all sort of terrible things about us."

"Well, they could be just a teensy bit irritated, Frank being dead and all."

"Don't make light of this, Bernie!" she snapped and I knew I'd played the wrong card.

"Whoa, whoa." If one could actually lay rubber backpedalling there'd have been a big black stripe in the street. "I'll do everything I can. I'll just tell them I need the time."

"Good. I'll see you then." I snapped the phone shut and dropped it in my pocket. My irritation quickly gave way to a veneer of determination that she was right: I deserved a couple of hours off to take care of my family. I'd be back in plenty of time for whatever TBC and his lawyer cooked up.

I turned to head toward my car where I could get warm and catch a tune while waiting for the next live shot when a dark sedan with a crumpled fender and a dangling tail light flung itself around the corner a block away and shouldered into an illegal parking spot in front of a fire hydrant. Call it my Spider-sense or maybe a glimmer of the common variety, but I backed up into the shadow of a building overhang as the door of the car burst open and Agent Semyenovic got out.

Chapter Twenty-one

I pressed myself hard against the side of the building and risked only a peek around the corner. Semyenovic looked this way and that like a bull eager to grind the matador's bones. I even thought I could see him snorting in the winter air. He must have heard my live shot and was zeroing in.

I made a quick review of my options:

1) Go over and have a chat with Semyenovic, appeal to his better nature, evidence of which was so far invisible.

2) Call the cops. And tell them, what? That an FBI agent was after me. They'd offer to help HIM.

3) Call TBC. And have him arrange a nice funeral.

4) Make myself scarce.

Sold.

I took off north on 33rd Street toward Chestnut and cut into an alley. Even though my car was in the other direction on Walnut, so was Agent Orange. My pace was a little faster than a jog so as not to attract attention that would attract him. I looked back. No sign, yet, so I pounded away. I was trying to think but ideas slipped through my mind like vapors. I didn't want to duck into a building and risk becoming trapped there, but I had to get off the street.

If he got back in his car, he could cruise around and spot me in a Philadelphia minute.

I dodged traffic in a very ill advised crossing of Chestnut Street which at this hour resembled an upscale drag strip with Acuras and Lexuses (or is it Lexi?) streaming toward Center City off to the east. I risked death once again crossing 33rd and then went along the sidewalk for nearly another block to where in the middle of a mini-park were stairs down into the earth.

Casting a quick glance over my shoulder, I hoped this would do the trick and thumped two steps at a time toward the underground trolleys below. The Subway-Surface cars, as they are called, are modern light rail vehicles that ran on streets through much of West and Southwest Philadelphia, but all five routes collected on tracks that took them first under University City and then alongside the Market-Frankford El, under the Schuylkill River to 13th St. on the far side of City Hall.

Half a dozen people were on the low platform when I arrived and I did what any SEPTA rider did, stuck my head out over the tracks and peek for an on-coming headlights. There was a glare in the darkness and the rumble of a trolley approaching. It emerged into the station with another illuminating the tunnel only a couple hundred feet behind it.

I tried not to bowl over the other customers but hustled up the steps, flashed a fare card and slipped into a seat near the back. Just as I was ready to exhale my terror, I saw Agent Semyenovic skid to a stop on the platform 20 or 30 feet behind. I ducked down, hoping he hadn't seen me, but from the way he glared at the trolley as it squealed around a tight turn, it wasn't a good bet.

Come on, come on, I thought. Faster, faster, must go faster. My body heaved forward spasmodically, as if I could urge my steed to some greater speed. If we could only get to 30th Street station before the next trolley had line of sight, I could disappear up the steps.

That was as far as my planning got.

We lurched down an incline onto the rails alongside the El. The upcoming station with the train platform in the center and the trolley stops on either side shined like sunrise. The entire tunnel shuddered as a westbound El lumbered out, sparks flaring from its power paddles as it crossed a switch.

My trolley stopped, maddeningly, right at the threshold of the station until a signal light changed from red to amber. We pulled in to the forward berth and I cast a backward look. The second trolley with a dark FBI-agent-like silhouette leaning over its dash, was just outside.

I leapt for the door, which fan-folded open when my foot fell on a step. I hit the ground, legs churning, up the stairs into the concourse level of the 30th Street transit station. I could run up another flight of steps to the street, or down steps to the El platform.

Approaching thunder and a breath of train-pushed wind made my decision and I sprinted 30 feet across the mezzanine and then downward as the silver El stopped with a hiss of air brakes. A quick flick of my eyes found Semyenovic vaulting up the steps from his trolley and without a speck of hesitation following me. I hit the platform as people disgorged from the train and I must have been looking over my shoulder because I plowed into a tweedy woman burdened with a briefcase and backpack. We both went down as she yelped but I tore myself to my feet.

"Doors are closing," said the ubiquitous recorded El announcement and I leaped for them, too late. They had shushed shut leaving me effectively dead in the water, or just dead.

"Freeze, FBI!" shouted the voice I most did not want to hear.

"Really," said the woman picking herself up off the platform, "it was just an accident."

I looked past her where Semyenovic had his gun aimed straight for me, perhaps only the presence of the woman staying his trigger finger. "Get down! On the ground, now!" I clapped my hands on the back of my head but did not lie down. Even though there were witnesses and

I hadn't even been shot, I was already beginning to see my life flash before my eyes, just to beat the rush.

The platform was half empty but those commuters within earshot retreated only far enough so as to not miss the show, and clattering down the steps came a SEPTA cop. My hero...

He saw Semyenovic's gun and drew his own. "Easy there, mister. Let's put down the hardware."

The agent lowered the barrel calmly. "I'm FBI. This man is under arrest."

"Officer," I yelled. "He's a stone cold loony. He already took a shot at me this morning over on City Line." I didn't want to overplay my hand by saying he was also trying to frame my boss for arson. That "loony" label could work both ways.

"Look," said Semyenovic, suddenly all reasonable. "Let me put the gun down and get out my badge." At the officer's almost imperceptible nod, he squatted slowly and placed a nasty-looking 9-millimeter pistol where everyone could see it.

"Arrest him!" I shouted.

"You shut up," said the officer, making the point with a twitch of his gun.

Semyenovic reached into a coat pocket and, with exaggerated care, withdrew his credentials which he flipped open. The effect was instantaneous. The cop's gun went from pointing midway between Semyenovic and me, to just at me.

"Sorry, agent. What do we have here?"

"A federal matter, none of your concern."

"I better call this in." The officer reached for the radio microphone clipped on his jacket lapel. It was the last move he'd ever make.

Semyenovic snatched a second gun from his pocket, my boss's hoary old revolver, and shot the SEPTA officer in the head.

The station exploded in action. The officer toppled back, bloody and unrecognizable. People screamed and stampeded, sometimes away from the violence, sometimes, confused by the echoing acoustics, toward it. The woman dropped back to the deck and I charged into Semyenovic, hitting him like an Eagles linebacker should finish off a blitz.

He oofed and went down. I swatted the revolver out of his hand and it skittered off onto the El tracks four feet below. He aimed an elbow that knocked my head back, broke a couple teeth and filled my mouth with blood. I went with the flow rolling off him and kicking his 9-mill off the other side of the platform.

I grabbed the dead cop's gun but Semyenovic shouldered me off into thin air. My arms pinwheeled as I fell and I landed with a breath-expelling thud, the police pistol nowhere near. Fireflies flickered across my vision as he produced yet another gun (How many did this guy have?) but I had other problems, a vibration off the tracks and a rising wind told me that something heavy this way comes, the westbound El with its gleaming white eyes rushing up from its river crossing.

I threw myself away from the platform and the third rail that ran beneath it as a shot rang out and the train, its horn bleating uselessly, thundered past like a 48 blade guillotine. Not pausing even to count my remaining limbs, I twisted through a gap in the fence separating the train and trolley tracks. For an instant I considered running up the steps but people were swirling like disturbed hornets, and the cops were coming, no doubt to shoot first, once they got a look at the dead guy.

Two things happened at once. My phone rang in my pocket and another gunshot rang out, pinging off a support beam. I ducked and looked back, to find Semyenovic in the El car, having fired through its now spider-web-cracked window. I took off on the trolley track bed toward Center City.

Bedlam continued behind me as more police arrived and SEPTA personnel tried to figure out if I'd gotten smooshed. I ducked between two pillars as a flurry of flashlights behind me indicated they'd ceased to think I was deceased. A trolley rolled past just a few inches from me and I took off again, down the incline under the Schuylkill.

"Hey, hey, come back!" someone yelled, but it didn't seem directed at me. "Henry, Henry, we have people in the tunnel. Shut it down! The El, the trolleys, shut it down!"

Thirty thousand morning commuters were just going to love me, assuming I lived long enough to feel their pain.

My only hope was to keep dodging in and out of the pillars which provided what modest cover there was and head for the 23rd Street station on the trolley tracks where I could get the hell out of there.

I swear I could hear Semyenovic closing in behind me but a stray thought was that I'd probably never hear the bullet that got me, having forgotten my Kevlar vest and all.

I reached the bottom of the incline, directly under the river where the tracks, ties and concrete base proved uncomfortably damp and I started up the other side alert for bullets from behind and trains and trolleys from ahead. An approaching rumble stilled but I recoiled between supports until I realized that. A few moments more and I came face to front with a westbound El train, lit only by emergency lights from within, but it filled the tunnel so that I had to sidestep back to the trolley side. There too was a disabled electric beast, its plug effectively pulled, and I was sidling past in the narrow space between trolley and wall, when I looked back. A dark figure hove into view from the El tracks and I waddled sideways like Charlie Chaplin, faster, faster.

The Agent was closing quickly and I ducked around the back of the trolley just as a shot pinged off its side, puckering the sheet metal. That round may have saved my life because it ignited the second subway panic of the last five minutes. Trolley passengers boiled from the vehicle as fast as they could given the close confines. I could hear the driver pleading with them to just get down and stay put, but some bulled through the front and rear doors anyway, clogging the small space like putty around a window.

I took that as a hint and bolted for the lights ahead, the 23rd Street trolley stop. There was another gunshot behind me, and screams.

"Down, down, FBI!" Semyenovic was yelling.   I lunged for the platform, around a corner and out of the line of fire, and slammed right into the bulletproof vest-clad chest of an on-coming policeman. He oofed, I oofed, then he and his six colleagues aimed their guns at me.

"On the floor!" one hissed. This time, I complied. Risking a sideward glance with my face on the concrete, I saw one of them peek down the tunnel and retreat. He held up one finger to the rest and then opened his palm. Wait, wait for it.

Agent Semyenovic charged into the station in pursuit of me and skidded to a halt, six police weapons on him. His eyes flicked from them to me.

"Drop that gun now!" ordered a cop sergeant. From the telepathy of eye contact, Semyenovic and I shared a what-the-fuck moment: then he raised his pistol and was shredded under a hail of police bullets.   I pulled up reflexively into an almost fetal position as the odor of gunpowder settled over me and the echo of the shots danced away.

One of the cops slapped me in handcuffs immediately and hauled me to my feet as the sergeant spoke into his microphone, something about the situation being under control, no injuries to police. At least here, I thought grimly.

They guided me with exaggerated gentleness to the stairs and we climbed up onto Market Street. A huge crowd of people was gawking from behind the police cordon and overhead I could hear the thump-thump-thump of TV helicopter rotors. My perp walk. Looks great on a resume, even if I hadn't done anything but save my own so-called life.

My phone rang in my pocket again, but I didn't have a free hand to answer and it soon went to voicemail.

I was loaded into the back of a police car for the second time in two days. Maybe I could get frequent rider miles. The car eased off into a street cleared of vehicles, then around a police cruiser turned 90 degrees to the flow of traffic and warning with its red and blue light show that a detour was in effect.

I watched all this absently, wondering if the driver would take me down Race Street or use the Vine Street expressway for one short exit. This time of day, it was a crapshoot, but when he hit his siren and the lights, it all became moot. Other vehicles melted to the side of the road and we, while not exactly zooming, ignored speed laws and traffic signals on the way to police headquarters, the Roundhouse.

The Roundhouse was some architect's wet dream. Take the Olympic symbol, those five interlocking rings, and knock two of them off. Now grow the remaining three rings into squat office block cylinders and you have the Roundhouse, where those enforcing the straight and narrow of the law walked crooked corridors and there was no such thing as a corner office because there were no corners.

I was piloted into the prisoner unloading area in the basement, then removed from the car with the same kid gloves. I must have been in shock because it never occurred to me, the old bromide, how many officers does it take to throw a prisoner down a flight of steps? None, he tripped.

My escort and I got in an elevator and rode up a couple of floors, took a right, a left and then through a door into a medium-sized room. There was small table, a couple of cheap office chairs and a curtain along one wall that probably concealed some one-way glass.

The officer removed my handcuffs and invited me to sit, which I did gratefully. He asked if I wanted a soda or coffee. I chose a diet cola and he, the good cop, left to fetch it.

He returned after a while and then left me alone with my caffeine fix. I suspected the door was locked but didn't bother testing it. Where would I go?

Time passed. The soda finished, I got up and peeked behind the curtain and, yes, it was a window into the lineup room, judging from the height markers along the wall. It was empty save for a couple of chairs.

My phone rang and reminded me that it had done so when I was preoccupied. I rescued it from my pocket.

"Gaston here."

"'Gaston here?'" mocked the voice at the other end. "Beanie, where the fuck are you?" It was Silcox. "All hell broke loose at 30th Street Station!   A cop shot, a chase in the subway and, for God's sake, another dead guy. Where have you been?"

"Oh," I said mildly, "standing on the El platform when the guy shot the cop, chased down the tunnel by the guy who shot the cop shooting at me, and then handcuffed by the cops after they blew the guy away. I'm in a police interrogation room now, so if you don't mind...."

"Fuck.." said Silcox, stretching the word out longer than any of his love-making. At least, that's what I'd heard. Then he recovered, "Bernie, I'm rolling. Tell me what happened."

I froze. Cops, corpse, computer, confidentiality, where do I begin? I needed a fucking lawyer. Or a Journalism Ethics professor.

"Don't swear, Bernie, for God's sake, I can't use any of that."

Oops, must have been thinking out loud. "I was on the 30th Street El platform when a man claiming to be an FBI agent pulled a gun on me and then shot a SEPTA police officer in the head when he tried to call the situation in. The officer never had a chance. I tackled the guy but he pushed me off on to the El track where I nearly got crushed by a train. He was shooting at me, forget all the people he might have hit, and I took off down the tunnel, dodging trolleys, trains and bullets until I got to the 23rd Street station where the police arrested me and shot him. DOTS, dead on the scene."

"And you're all right?" He sounded more astonished than relieved.

"Happens all the time. Usually, I'm wearing spandex. Now I'm in the Roundhouse awaiting questioning."

"Whoa, whoa, whoa. You mean to tell me two guys are dead in a gunfight in the El tunnel and you're our inside guy and what you're inside is the Roundhouse?"

"Pretty much.   By the way, I'm not coming in. And tell TBC, when you see him, to call off his AWOL lawyer."

"What lawyer?"

"Just tell him."

When I heard a sound behind me I quickly dropped the curtain, palmed the phone and plopped back into my seat.

The door opened and Captain Pell stepped into the room.

"You are a fucking piece of work," he said.

"You have no idea," I replied.

Chapter Twenty-two

Unhurriedly, Pell "invited" me to sit, pulled up a chair opposite me and carefully placed a bulging file folder on the table between us. This was a different Captain Pell than I had seen in Frank's house or on the street. This was a bear in its den, confident, even smug, that he had control of the situation.

I was his toy. Just so long as I wasn't his chew toy.

"I'd like to ask you some questions to help sort things out."

"Do I need a lawyer?"

"I don't know. Do you?" He set a pad and pen next to the supersized file. "Do you have anyone in mind?" I thought about the debacle of my deposition. I didn't even know whom I was supposed to have had. TBC had said his own lawyer was in Colorado.

I shook my head. "Look," Pell said, twirling the point of his pen on the pad, "Ask yourself this question, did you do anything wrong? If the answer is yes, call a lawyer. If it's no, let's talk. Maybe you can get out of here sooner rather than later."

Great, I thought. Asking for my lawyer makes me guilty of "something". All he'd have to do is figure out what. Almost against my better judgment, I nodded and said, "Ask away."

"Did you kill Officer Masterson, the SEPTA cop?"

"No! It was that lunatic FBI agent! I think he took a shot at me over on City Line at a diner this morning! Hit somebody else!"

Pell made a note. "But you didn't stick around."

I refused to feel guilty about that. "No, I didn't. I went back...." I paused. How much should I be saying about Nash, the break-in, the investigation, the arson? "I drove off, okay. Let's leave it at that."

"You know," said Pell, turning a page on his pad, "I'm actually not investigating any of that. Someone else will be in to talk to you, once they finish processing the scene." And cleaning up the mess, I'd wager.

I kept my mouth shut. Answer what's asked was the rule I'd adopted.

"I'm still looking into your brother-in-law's death. There are a few things that don't add up." The loose ends, the loose kind, he had mentioned yesterday.

"Such as."

He moved the folder halfway across the table and flipped it open. It was filled with photographs, the top one of snowy footprints. "The Crime Scene Unit took these the night Officer Tierney was murdered. I think we even saw them out the back window while they were doing it." I nodded. So far, no disagreement.

"Well, this is all digital stuff, very high megapixel resolution which they analyzed in some fancy computer they have in the lab. Look what they found." He flipped out a second photo of a single footprint identical as far as I could tell to the rest.   "You see here the tread mark? They used some shadow enhancing gizmo to bring it out a bit, but it's there. You see it, right?"

I merely nodded.

"Hmmph," Pell pulled out yet another photo, this one of a pair of police boots laced tight on a pair of police feet,

Frank's, there on the floor of his living room. "Notice anything?"

I studied the picture, feeling a perverse touch of test anxiety. Would I get the right answer? I looked for maybe a minute before I gave up.

"Beats me. Not to be crass, but it looks like a pair of dead man's boots."

"Indeed. Look at the treads." He swiveled the pictures around until the soles and boot prints were parallel. There was no doubt. They had different patterns.

"Here's another puzzler. I want you to look here along the right edge." He tapped the footprint photo with his pen. "You see that slight stair step effect?" I could. It was faint and I didn't know what it meant.

"Here's what we think made that, one person walking through the same snowy tracks twice, and not quite getting the footwork quite right." He gave me a piercing look, as if this were some sort of revelation that would cause me to crumble. Oh, yes, yes, you got me. I shot Frank to death with his pistol when I was 30 miles away during a blizzard. It was a hell of shot, but I'd been practicing. And then I walked to the garage twice, just to say I could.

"Okay, twice," I said. "So what?"

"'What' is that the story Jan Tierney tells us is that Frank went out to the garage to get his baseball bat, came back in and whacked her on the arm. That's when she shot him. Bing, bang, boom. Why would Frank, in a fit of rage, have gone to the garage twice, and changed his boots?"

I had no answer. Who could? Frank was beyond the reach of any questioning but Madam Zelda's at the state fair.

"This is the X-ray on Mrs. Tierney's arm." Pell turned it slightly and held it up toward the ceiling lights so that by craning my neck we could both see. "Right here," he poked the picture with his pen point, "is the fracture." I had to take his word for it. I was lucky if I could read traffic signals, let alone X-rays. "Notice how fine it is, hairline they called it."

"Okay," I responded noncommittally.

Away went the X-ray and out came a copy of a bill, which he spun toward me so I could follow along.

"See, this is Frank and Jan's cable statement from last month. Here's basic. Here's HBO. Here's landline phone. Here's cable modem, none of which is in the least bit unusual," he paused for a dramatic sigh, "except they didn't have a computer."

"Of course, they had a computer!" I snapped. "Jen said it was broken or something. I took it to a repair place. What do you do, go through everybody's bills?"

"Money is often a powerful motive," Pell replied although his tone said, but not in this case. "Give me a minute, will you? I have to set something up." He rose and left the room. I twiddled, fiddled and would have diddled but, hey, it's fucking police headquarters. Have some respect.

When Pell returned in a few minutes, but here again it seemed like forever, he went to the curtains and pulled them back. Now, instead of an empty lineup room, and its Spartan furnishings were a cart on which sat a computer and monitor tended by Detective Dellacourt and, in a chair looking as pissed as I've ever seen her, Jen.

"What's going on here?" I demanded.

"Patience," said Pell as he wagged a finger at me. He punched a button on an intercom. "Go ahead, Jimmy. Let 'er rip."

I was dimly aware that Dellacourt was fiddling with the computer, which actually looked a lot like the "broken" computer, bringing up the OS desktop, but Pell stood in my way.

"We got a call from a friend of yours, Oliver Osteen."

"Frank and Jan's computer..."

"The very one. Don't blame him. He was very conflicted but he had to call us."

"Why?"

"You'll see." Pell slid out of the way and I walked up to the window to get a better look. In a moment, I didn't want one. The images that were on that screen, I don't even want to describe, but it was kiddy porn. No, that's not vile enough an expression. It was child pornography, repulsive scenes that Dellacourt flicked through using the mouse. Yuck, yuck, ick, OMG. I turned to Pell.

"Look," he commanded. Click, click, click and when the slideshow stopped on a particular image, I wished for blindness so that I had not seen, could not see, what was there on the monitor. It was my nephew Frankie, many months younger, dressed in some stupid police or bus driver's vest, the type a really tiny Chippendale might wear. He was sucking on a banana.

Only it wasn't a banana.

Chapter Twenty-three

I think I shrieked like a dame in a 50's horror movie. My legs gave out and I ended up kneeling, looking through the window, transfixed by the photo of my nephew's abuse and the thought crossed my mind that maybe I would have been better off letting Semyenovic shoot me.

On the other side of the glass, Jen buried her head in her hands and wept but was not, as far as I could tell, surprised.

After a moment, Pell tucked his hand under my right arm and helped me up. "Come on," he said, "let's go meet the girls."

We went out in the hallway where we saw Jen being escorted by Dellacourt. She looked at me with a mixture of contempt and fury. "I told you to throw the damn thing away," she hissed. "Where were you when I called? That horrid woman from Children's Services came by early, accompanied by police. She took all the kids! I ended up here."

Our parade ended in a third room, where, at a conference table, sat Jan in an orange prison jumpsuit, Lisette Hanratty in a black wool skirt suit, and the Police Commissioner and the D.A. in their professional finery. Jen made eye contact with her twin and mouthed something that I read as, "They know." Jan gave one curt nod.

Jen and I took the two empty seats while Pell and Dellacourt assumed sentry posts by the door, as if bolting had ever entered my mind. Well, actually it had, but only in an "I sure wish I were anywhere else" sort of way. D.A. Rittenhouse, looked over top of glasses perched midway down his nose, tapped a pen that sounded like a gavel in this stillness.

"Well," he began, "the situation has changed somewhat since the last time I addressed this case." He cast a piercing look at Hanratty whose response gave nothing away. "We have several ways to proceed. We believe that new information casts the murder of Officer Frank Tierney in a completely different light, but a light that is not without its own difficulties. Option one: we charge Jan Tierney with first degree murder and the usual long list of additional counts."

"Nonsense," Hanratty interrupted but quieted when Rittenhouse held up his index finger. He turned to Jen.

"You, Mrs. Gaston, would also be charged with first degree murder inasmuch as we believe you facilitated the homicide. Under the law, it's the same as if you had pulled the trigger."

"I wish I had," she muttered.

"Hush!" said Hanratty.

"You...." the D.A. locked his gaze on me, held it for a moment, and then waved a hand dismissively. "You helped us break this case, but your involvement in this morning's bloodshed," Jen and Jan both stared at me, "will take some sorting out.

"Yet, going to trial would clearly be a mess. We believe the two of you," indicating Jan and Jen, "killed Officer Tierney because of the child pornography in general and the use of little Frankie in it in particular. Airing this in court would create a media circus that makes what we've had so far look like afternoon tea. It would devastate your family, the Tierney family and besmirch all the fine men and women who work in the police department.

"So here's what I propose. You, Mrs. Tierney, will enter a guilty plea to a general charge of murder..."

"Absolutely not!" snapped Hanratty. "No jury in the world will convict her. They will give her a medal for killing that scumbag."

"Perhaps so," Rittenhouse went on evenly, "but at what cost? Think for a moment about what I said. Even if we managed to keep these photos secret during the run-up to trial, and a lot of them were downloaded from the Internet so the ones of Frankie could already be out there in cyberspace, we will have to show them in court. Is that what you want, damaging the children yet again."

"You want to send their mother to jail," protested Hanratty. "That's pretty damaging."

"She chose this path, Lisette, as much as her husband chose his. There were other ways to go besides murder, people to tell about his crimes."

"Like who?" Jan spat, "The police? Internal Affairs? Cops don't turn on cops, don't turn in cops. It's the blue brotherhood, sweep it up, cover it up, make it go away. Cops think they can get away with anything."

The Commissioner shifted uncomfortably but did not rise to the defense of his department or his profession. A man of few words, that.

Rittenhouse tapped his pen. "I appreciate the passion of your conviction although I do not agree. It is moot, however. The damage has been done. If I may continue..." He awaited subdued nods from around the table.

"You would plead guilty to a general charge of murder, as a show of remorse. We will stipulate that you get minimal jail time, probably 7 to 10 years."

"Outrageous!" Hanratty again. She should take quiet lessons from the Commissioner. "Three to six years away from her children."

"And them without their father forever. Murder creates a debt to society that must be paid, Lisette, even the murder of a son-of-a-bitch. So, seven to ten years for you," pointing at Jan, "but with you," pointing at Jen, "we need to be creative. I think community service is the way to go, off the books, of course. I think two thousand hours. That's about one year's work, forty hours a week, donated to the betterment of a society you have wronged."

Blood drained from Jen's face and she choked.

"But before we proceed, I need the truth from you both."

"No way." Hanratty again. "You want them to confess."

"To what end, Lisette?" Rittenhouse spread his hands. "An official confession is exactly what I don't want because it leads right back to our dilemma..."

There was a polite cough from Pell. "Excuse me, Mr. Rittenhouse, but how about we do this? How about I reconstruct the crime from what we know and what we believe. No one is confessing to anything."

There were no objections, even from Hanratty. "Go ahead," Rittenhouse said.

Pell tossed his fat folder on the table and began to pace slowly around the room. "Officer Tierney had been heavy into child pornography for at least a year, judging by the trail of uploads and downloads. He has a tidy collection of pictures locked deep in the hard drive. It took a computer technician diagnosing the hard drive to spot a huge block of memory in use, but not showing up in any of the usual places, so presumably Mrs. Tierney was none the wiser for a good long time. Well, a long time. Somehow, probably recently, she discovered the file and, needless to say, was appalled. She confided in her twin sister and, together, they concocted the murder scheme.

"The key to the plot was its timing. Our canvas of the neighborhood found that the people living next door on the right were in the Bahamas for two weeks and the old lady on the other side is nearly stone deaf. She has her TV on loud as a jackhammer almost all the time.

"The snowstorm would also serve to muffle the gunshots and keep the number of passersby down. When Officer Tierney phoned with his ETA home from work, Mrs. Tierney called Mrs. Gaston who put the kids to bed early, having slipped them a mickey. Oh, your mom didn't put it that way, but cold medicine to induce drowsiness? Sounds like a mickey to me.

"Officer Tierney arrived and was pretty quickly ambushed. Two shots to the torso, fatal almost instantly, but now the fun begins." Speaking of fun, Pell was clearly relishing his role as lecturer. "Mrs. Gaston arrived, but not out front. She pulled up behind the detached garage along the alley out back. Inside the garage she found a pair of Officer Tierney's boots, put them on and came into the house carrying a baseball bat that was stored there.

"Once in the house, she proceeded, while stepping around her brother-in-law's still-warm body, to whack Mrs. Tierney in the arm with the baseball bat. That's the reason the fracture is so minor. Had Officer Tierney hit her in a fit of rage, I am confident the bone would have been shattered, but sister hitting sister in this cover-up, neither could really muster the will to do much damage.

"Now to get rid of the other evidence, the computer. The ladies piled it into boxes, but Mrs. Gaston found it was too big to carry in one trip. So she made two, carefully, carefully, retracing her steps, hoping that the storm would mess up the scene and fool us. It almost did," he nodded toward the sisters as if in acknowledgement, "but little things didn't add up.

"The first was Mrs. Tierney's confession. Sure, it made my job easier but it seemed just a little too quick. Here's your murder and your ready-made suspect. So long. Don't let the door hit you on the way out. You were planning on, counting on that police don't like to air our dirty laundry.

"But, as I said, little things didn't add up. The tiny fracture, the footprints made by the wrong boots, just enough that I kept thinking, I'm missing something. It was only when the computer turned up that I knew what it was. You admitted to manslaughter to cover up something worse, like first-degree murder.

"How am I doing?"

Jen and Jan sat like stony bookends of silence.

"I think we get the idea," said the D.A. Pell nodded and returned to his post by the door. "The offer stands but it is a limited time offer. Once we leave this room, we will proceed to charge you both and let the chips fall where they may."

Jan looked from her sister to her lawyer and back. "Seven to 10 years," she said imploringly.

"Let me have a moment with my clients?" said Hanratty. As they ducked their heads together and whispered, I wondered whether it was a good idea, or even ethical, that she represent both. I was fresh out of other lawyers at the moment and, given the situation, the fewer who knew about this the better. After conferring, they pulled apart. "I want this in writing including the recommendation for three to six years. Can we count on the judge's cooperation and discretion?"

"The Judiciary is independent but we can present a compelling, albeit abbreviated case, that this serves the public's interest."

"But no guarantees?"

"No guarantees. I am taking a huge risk here, Lisette, using my discretion as District Attorney in a way that could blow up in my face. Discretion, now there's a word that applies all around, don't you think? I'll have someone draw up the plea deal by the end of the day."

"I want to do my time here in the city," said Jan. 'I don't want to be sent to the other side of the state."

Rittenhouse nodded. "I'll see what I can do. That might be out of my hands. We have an overcrowded prison system, as you know, and to make an exception for you may call unwanted attention to this case. You might consider whether having the kids visit you, anywhere, is in their best interests."

"I miss them so much," Jan blubbered, her lips shaking, shoulders drooping.

"C'est la vie," Rittenhouse replied. "C'est la mort."

No one asked me for my opinion, which would have been: what the fuck are you people talking about? That Jan shot Frank I'd already gotten used to. I'd put it in a mental dumpster called "things I'll never understand and don't want to think about." Now, given her complete lack of protest, it looked as if Jen, my beloved wife and helpmate, mother of our children, flower monger and person with whom you did NOT want to play Texas Hold-em (trust me on this) helped engineer a premeditated murder.

I decided I really had better put the toilet seat down from now on.

Rittenhouse packed up his papers and left as my mind kept repeating "Jen the accomplice, Jen the accomplice." Lisette Hanratty was saying something. She patted each woman's hands and I was looking at killer hands, gun-gripping, trigger-pulling fingers, bat-wielding, computer-removing alibi-producing hands.

In a way, I couldn't blame them. The moment I saw that picture of little Frankie I could have pulled the trigger too, at least right then when I was enraged, but Jan and Jen had thought this out, schemed to commit murder and, if not exactly cover up the crime, cover up the motive.

I looked at them both, the formerly identical twins who were suddenly strangers. Why didn't Jen tell me, I wondered? And if she had, what then? Maybe, given the bizarre logic of what they had done, I was better off ignorant.

Except, of course, for the computer. Had I known what was on it, I would have smashed it myself. Or scrounged around the station for one of those industrial strength degaussers we used to erase tapes back in the day. One of them would screw up that hard drive but good, flat-lining its obscene collection of 1's and 0's.

Leaving only the pictures Frank may have uploaded like someone trading perverted collectable cards on the WWW, worldwide weirdoes. Frankie, my little man, the plaything of the wretched.

Someone was talking to me and I discovered it was the Commissioner. It's alive! It's alive!

"Mr. Gaston, we're going to need to question you about the other matters, the p'lice officer's death and the FBI agent's, and the shooting at the diner."

Jen and Jan looked at me as if they too had just met someone they didn't recognize, someone with blood on his hands. Mine was just splatter, though.

"Here?" I wondered lamely.

"Yes, in a little while. City and Lower Merion p'lice, SEPTA and the FBI all at once. It could speed things up."

I nodded, realizing that I was exhausted, not just tired, nor bone-weary, but like a hot-air balloon once the burner is turned off, collapsing, sagging inward with a long low sigh.

"Whatever, " I shrugged.

Hanratty rose, as did Jen and Jan. The sisters embraced with the desperate clutch of two people falling from a very high place. After a moment, Dellacourt put Jan in handcuffs and released her to a female officer who ushered her out. She cast a fleeting glance back as she disappeared around the corner and Jen crumbled into her seat. When I put my arm around her, she huddled against me, shuddering with tears.

I wanted to whisper some sort of solace, like "It'll be all right" but I had no faith that it would be. All I could do is rock her gently and wonder what to do next.

Chapter Twenty-four

Next sort of took care of itself. Lisette Hanratty quietly conferred with Jen for a little while longer and offered, no, suggested, that she retain her own counsel. There was no conflict between Jen and Jan's stories now but who knew? Jen nodded blankly and did not seem to have reached a decision by the time the door opened and an officer announced that the investigators were ready for me.

They took me down a floor to a better-appointed interview room where a suit convention was in progress. There were FBI suits, SEPTA suits, city police detective suits, suburban police detective suits and probably a few male models just looking for work.

A Crime Scene Unit tech swabbed my hands for gunshot residue and they took my winter jacket for processing. They offered me another soda, which I declined because unless they also wanted a urine sample as well I figured I'd better slow down. The short walk had lifted my lethargy somewhat but, you know, after the events of the morning, and frankly the middle of the night that preceded it,

I was almost ready to confess to the Lindbergh baby kidnapping if it got me a nap.

Before things started, there was a rap at the door and an officer ushered in yet another suit, but this was a cut above, high-end, Italian-designed, draped on the trim frame of a lawyer sent to represent me. He introduced himself all around, F. Bruce Kleiner of one of the biggest law firms in the city, and then in a hushed consultation with me said he'd been hired by TBC to watch over our interests. Maybe he actually said "your interests". I gave him the discount version of this morning's thrill ride and he asked some pithy questions like, "Did you ever touch the gun?"

I had, of course, touched A gun but it ended up on the El tracks unfired.

The session became pretty much a blur for me. I told my story chronologically from this morning, although without any mention of the break-in at TBC's manse or the likely provenance of the fourth gun, the one which Nash had conveniently forgotten to register. I told them of Semyenovic's interest in TBC, the deposition in which the agent had tried to connect Nash with the arson fire and the agent's agitated appearance outside the D.A.'s office during the demonstration.

If harrumphing were coffee, that place would have been a Starbucks with me as the barista serving up cup after cup of disquiet. The FBI guys took only a brief stab at trying to show that their fellow wasn't off his rocker but even without knowing about the break-in, the gas can and the stolen gun, it was obvious he had been calling his own plays.

Preliminary ballistics results were that TBC's secret gun had been used in the diner shooting. The victim was going to need some major physical therapy, by the way. He almost lost the arm.

The tech came back with the verdict that I had not fired a gun, which seemed to disappoint almost everyone because this was one stinkpot of a mess. I saw lurking in the back of the room the FBI agent in charge of public affairs. He seemed to be working on a migraine because shortly he was going to have to go outside the Roundhouse and tell the assembled media horde (Even though I had not been near a window, I knew they were there) what happened. There's no way that was going to look good on his resume, or the six o'clock news.

The police public affairs guy, however, seemed to be enjoying himself, displaying a quiet smirk and popping breath mints. In the Big Leagues, there's nothing better than being able to pass the buck.

The interrogation petered out about 3 p.m. when they seemed to have exhausted ways to try to trap me. It was with obvious great reluctance that they said I was free to go. They returned my coat and I shook Kleiner's hand. We were shown the door, escorted through the maze to the main entrance where a couple of reporters and cameramen lurked just inside the foyer to escape the cold.

Seeing me, they quickened like wolves on a fresh scent, and the gang bang assembled outside on a concrete patio around a bouquet of microphones blossoming from a light stand set up by one of the TV guys. Gina stood off to the side, her mike clipped in with the rest this time. Kleiner went first, explaining just for the record that I had not been charged and, in fact, had done nothing wrong. Even while he was speaking, I felt all the electronic eyes on me, my second taste of my own medicine in two days. Yuck.

I could have kept my mouth shut and let them quote WPN or "sources" the rest of the day, but I knew how these things work. If you run, they chase. Imagine the video of them pursuing me through the Roundhouse parking lot. I'd look guilty. Heck, if they chased the Pope, he'd look guilty. So I gave them a bone.

I played it as straight as I had with the cops, which is to say I gave the sanitized version of the encounter in the El station, the murder, the chase and the police fusillade that had ended it. When reporters asked, why, I told them I didn't know, which was technically true. I had no idea what motivated Semyenovic to take his investigation so far out of bounds but I'd leave it to the authorities to reveal just how out of bounds it had been. They too might choose to be coy.

 After about five minutes, as questioning degenerated into the what had I had for breakfast sort (which reminded me I was famished), the police and FBI spokesmen emerged. Saved by the badge, twice in one day.

 Kleiner and I strolled off, just me and the boss's gunslinger. He'd come over by cab from one of the Center City skyscrapers that only sky-high billable hours could afford, and was planning to hail one for the return trip. Only then did it occur to me that I'd left my car at a meter in University City, what, about a month ago and you probably couldn't even see the windshield any more for all the tickets.

 Kleiner chuckled when I told him that. "Come on," he said, "we'll get you squared away." It's amazing how quickly a guy in a cashmere coat, carrying a brief case, could grab a cab in this town. In a moment, Kleiner and I were being squired west on Arch Street by Hassan or Hussein or some other recent import who probably knew where Mecca was but had a little trouble with 35th and Walnut.

 Sure enough there were enough citations to make a ticket-tape parade but the car hadn't been towed at least. As the cab idled nearby, I harvested the bumper crop. Kleiner laughed again (I guessed I was just an amusing guy) and relieved me of the problem.

 "I know someone at traffic court," he said, "who ought to be able to make these disappear." There was a lot of that going on. "After all, it's tough to feed your meter when you're in custody helping solve the murder of a police officer." He clapped me on the shoulder and shook my hand as he got back in the taxi, which pulled away.

 I realized with a start that I should have checked for my keys but they were still in my coat pocket, tucked under the gloves. I started the engine and was all set to pull into traffic myself when I wondered where I was going. That was both a practical and philosophical concern. I flipped open the phone and called Jen's cell. No answer. I called home. No answer. I called the station. Carrie answered.

"If it isn't the news lightning rod," she said. "Remind me never to get on an airplane with you."

"And here I was thinking, Cancun in January is supposed to be lovely. What's going on?"

"Well, it's all you, all the time. Everybody is all over this subway shooting of yours..."

"Not mine. I was shot at, remember."

"Semantics. The TV's have just done news bulletins from the Roundhouse with your face featured. You're going to have to join the Screen Actors Guild."

"Or Victims Anonymous. Listen, I've had quite a day. I hope you guys can live without me."

"Your reporting, sure, but what are you going to do for an encore tomorrow? We'll need a new top story."

This was getting me nowhere. "Can you get a message to TBC? He and I should talk."

"He's in. I'll transfer you. But, just a second, that guy from the MLK foundation, called back. He's getting pretty irritated you guys aren't connecting."

"I'll catch him on Monday at one of the day of service events. I'm all out of bullets now."

"Throw your recorder at him. I'll transfer you to TBC." There were a couple of beeps and rings.

"Warren Nash," TBC's voice came on the line.

"Bernie Gaston."

"Mr. Problem-solver!" he positively gushed. "I just got off the phone with the Feds. They're suddenly all blush-blush apologetic about Semyenovic. Nothing but assurances that I am no longer the target of an investigation. I'm not sure I believe it but I'll buy you a drink anyway."

"I'll take a rain check, if you don't mind. It's been a trying day."

"And now he's the master of understatement. Bernie, if you want to get anywhere in this business, you have to get out there, toot your own horn." Here, I thought I already had gotten somewhere. WPN, for all its faults, was far better than the 5,000-watt daytimer I'd worked out in Junction City Colorado with its emphasis on agricultural news. Before that, I'd had no idea farms could smell so many different ways, all of them bad.

"Well, I'll do the talk shows tomorrow but I really have to go home now."

"Sure, sure, go get some rest. How about, take the weekend off! I'll let the gang know you'll be in on Monday."

"God willing," I replied and clicked off. I squinted out into stretching shadows of this very long, very short day. It was momentarily peaceful but then I saw a suspicious movement in my side mirror, a parking enforcement officer with ticket printer at the ready. Gotta go.

My homeward drive in the early evening rush gave me close to an hour to think about my domestic situation. I loved Jen dearly but this could be the elephant in the room, her involvement in the murder, mine in solving it. Sometimes those elephants kept quiet. Sometimes they made noise. Sometimes they sat on you.

Chapter Twenty-five

My house looked quiet, nestled in a moth-eaten blanket of snow, as I pulled up. Jen's car was there and the living room light shown through sheer daytime drapes. I entered without ceremony but kid radar wasn't fooled. Elizabeth and Lorraine charged out from the back room and competed for first hugs, then second.

"We went for a ride with a nice lady," said Elizabeth. "She took us to a home where we had pizza and played. Samantha and Frankie are lucky. They get to stay."

Huh?

I hung up my coat and allowed myself to be dragged into the back room where Jen was cooking what smelled like spaghetti sauce, or gravy, if you're a South Philadelphian.

"We're down two kids," I said, trying to keep things light.

"Your girlfriend put them in a foster home." So much for light.

"What are you talking about?"

Instead of answering she put her spoon in a cup on the counter and hustled the kids out to the electronic babysitter which was tuned to a cable channel that promised to rot little minds much slower than the others. She turned the sound up to the point where normally she'd be yelling for them to turn it down. The girls were in hog heaven. I, apparently, was in someplace warmer.

"That Katrina Something-Italian," Jen resumed, returning to the kitchen and resumed stirring. "Come on, I saw you eyeing her over at Jan's house...that night. Pretty girl, stunning really. You have good taste." I almost blurted, I always have, you, or something equally Hallmark and desperate. "She's our caseworker now, well, Jan's. First, she shows up here this morning with the cops and scares the children half to death, packing them off to some safe house while they questioned me. Then when I go to get them back I find out that the Tierneys, Frank's family, has in fact filed for custody."

"But you're their aunt. Betty's their grandmother."

"And they have Grandma and Grandpa and a couple of their own aunts and uncles all of whom swear they'll take care of Sam and Frankie like their own."

"That's scary."

"Why?" Jen turned and crossed her arms, heedless of where the spoon flicked red sauce.

I leaned in. "Frank was a pervert. A lot of times that runs in families. Maybe somebody there did something to him."

"Oh, sweet Jesus," she sighed. "The kids have suffered enough."

"But we have a problem. Two, actually. You are the twin sister of Daddy's killer and we can't reveal why we think it's such a bad, bad idea the kids go with the Tierneys. Any whiff of kiddy porn and the whole house of cards comes down. We might gain the kids but lose you."

Jen went from forlorn to five-lorn or six-. I opened my arms to hug her and she accepted, even thinking to flick the spoon onto the stove before moving in close. We stayed entwined for a long moment, alone together. I breathed in the aroma of her hair, her skin, her worry, and felt at peace. All the other shit aside, this was where I belonged.

"BG," she sniffed, close to tears. "Why did he have to be such a bastard? Child pornography, with his own son? God, there might be shots of Sam too, taken when she was too young to remember. Jan showed me the pictures, file after file until I couldn't stand it anymore. I grew hot at first, angry hot, then cold, cold. Jan suggested killing him and I agreed. No hesitation, no remorse. I've cried having a pet dog put to sleep but this, nothing.

"When I saw his body on their floor, all I could think was, good fucking riddance. Me, cursing. That's what he did to me, ripped through my nice-girl exterior and let loose my monster. "

"You should have told me."

"It's easier to ask forgiveness than permission. Please, please, forgive me."

"Of course, my love," and I kissed her head. As long as we were on confessions, I said, "I'm sorry about the computer."

"Hush," she replied gently. "You did what Boy Scouts do. You help old ladies across the street, even if they don't want to go."

"You think I'm a Boy Scout?" I didn't know whether to be appalled or, well, appalled.

"You're my Boy Scout," she looked up and kissed me in a very arousing way, given that we were standing in the kitchen with the kids in the next room and all. "You get a merit badge." I could hardly wait for the award ceremony.

"Can I have more milk?" We looked down and there was Lorraine, hoisting her Sippy cup in our direction.

"May I," corrected Jen, all Mommy again. "Sure." She swept the cup up to the counter and refilled it while I tried to regroup.

"When is dinner going to be ready, hon?" I asked, back in Daddy mode.

"Only as long as it takes to cook the pasta. Say, fifteen minutes. Why?"

"You know what I was thinking?" I said in my broadcasting voice that cut through the TV chatter like a police siren. The girls looked over expectantly and I summoned them with a wave of my hands. I got down on my knees to welcome them in a group hug and Jen took the hint and did so too.

"I was thinking, after dinner, let's all go for ice cream." There were squeals of delight from two little mouths and a contented smile from Jen. "Just us," I said. "Just our family."

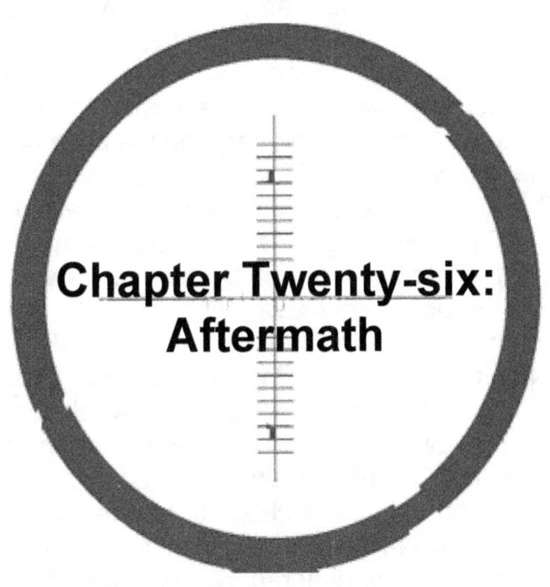

Chapter Twenty-six:
Aftermath

There were plenty of loose ends, the loose kind, after all this happened.

Jan's plea was accepted by a judge with minimal fuss, although Lisette Hanratty was just biting her tongue in court. She paced like a junk yard dog on a chain, longing to lunge, because she wanted to present the real defense, that Jan had done what any mother would do when she found out what had been done to her children by her own husband. But they crossed the T's and dotted the I's and Jan was hustled off to SCI Muncie, about an hour north of Harrisburg in the central part of the state. Since the only other women's prison (staying in Philadelphia didn't pan out) was 400 miles away near Erie, it could have been worse.

Frank's younger brother Lawrence and his wife Becky's bid for custody of Samantha and Frankie was jointly opposed by Betty, Jan and me. This threatened to get ugly. In addition to my worries that someone on the Tierney side of the family had molded Frank into being a deviant, we didn't want Jan to get out of prison only to find that her children had been turned against her by the relentless propaganda of a wounded clan. Betty, of course, did not know about our hidden reasons, but we managed to buff up her desire to have the kids more rather than less. We caught a break when Lawrence argued the case himself and made a mess of it.

The judge ruled the kids would live with Betty and see the Tierneys often in a complicated sharing arrangement evidently put out by someone who used to move trains through a freight yard.

About a week after "the incidents", as I like to think of them, if I think of them at all, I ran into Captain Pell on a job in Society Hill. This was going to make headlines, a randy 60-something playboy found dead, and naked, in his Florida room hot tub, nubile girlfriend unaccounted for.

Dellacourt strolled in close to the media holding pen and surreptitiously wiggled a finger at me. I waited a few moments and then meandered casually around a corner, following him. Pell sat half in, half-out of his car, chomping on a cigar.

"What's up?" I asked.

"Got some news for you about your FBI friend."

Well, this was unexpected. "Like what? He's still dead, I take it."

Pell gestured with the cigar. "Yeah, and he would have been anyway, I gather. After he was shot, they did an autopsy and found some interesting stuff, like some kind of growth in his brain."

"A tumor?"

"I don't know. Probably. Somebody might have said but was a long medical thing, sounded real serious."

"They think it made him crazy?"

"No, just desperate. He knew he was sick, and all the options bad," Pell snapped up fingers one by one, "With chemo you get sicker, with brain surgery maybe you get paralyzed or something, radiation's no picnic either and doing nothing, you're dead. Somebody a long time ago said, the prospect of the gallows focuses the mind. Think of it as a football metaphor. It's late in the game, you're down by two touchdowns. You might as well go long."

"It seemed a little more personal than calling a flea-flicker."

Pell shrugged. "As personal as the Eagles and Dallas? That could be. Anyway I thought you might want to know."

"Thanks," I said, then, "You know, this sounds like news, about the guy who shot a SEPTA cop."

"But not from you. I catch you anywhere near this story and I'll pin your ears back." And give me detention, too, I thought.

"Okay then, can you tell me anything about this job?"

He flicked his cigar ash in my direction. "Don't push your luck. Get back with the baying hounds and someone will come out when they come out."

"Hey, I had to give it a shot." I think he winked at me as I turned to go.

That was only the first surprise involving Captain Pell. The second occurred shortly thereafter.

The flower shop was on life-support after Frank's murder. With Jan in the "big house", cops went elsewhere for their make-up and break-up needs. Jen got some FTD business of course but, here too, the gallows cast its long shadow.

Then the phone rang and a certain Dolores Pell offered to buy the business. Yes, the Captain and his wife lived nearby in Morrell Park, and his missus was looking for a new avenue. They paid a fair price, better than they could have given how sales had flagged, and once the place was under new management, especially that of a captain's wife, customers managed to find it again.

Frank's dirty computer was a gold mine of information on perverts. The cops and the Feds used some IP addresses in it to dangle child pornography and several of the bastards took the bait. Some were across the country, one was down the block and there was a guy in Bangkok looking to set up a rendezvous. Who would name a city "Bangkok" anyway? What were they thinking?

Of course, I suppose the "City of Brotherly Love" can come up looking pretty tawdry too.

At work, I had a new best friend, Mr. Nash. After our strange little bonding experience and my nearly taking a bullet on his behalf, all of a sudden he was inviting me into his office for chats at least once a week. Truthfully, sometimes they got uncomfortable because he would touch on his business dealings and I got the feeling I was being groomed as an unindicted co-conspirator. I kept my squirming on the inside and TBC either didn't notice or didn't care because he loved to pontificate.

His nephew Lorne, by the way, ended up going back to school for a certificate in massage therapy. Insert joke here. Come on, it's just too easy.

We never did learn who set the warehouse fire although I was willing to bet on Agent Semyenovic. The Arson Squad kept its file open. The insurance company was mollified by settling for 40 cents on the dollar of the policy's inflated value. The city condemned the site and turned it into a community park, which served as a magnet for further REIT activity in the surrounding blocks.

Jen started her one-year of community service and with some gentle prodding from me found a halfway house for battered women that would take everything she was prepared to give. It was a real eye-opener to her, the trail of tears from the kind of domestic abuse that she and Jan had only pretended. Things were a little tight, what with Jen not bringing in a paycheck, but my BFF proved to be very generous.

The news business continued pretty much as it had before all of this. I'd cover a couple or three stories a day, cram as much as I could into the copy and forget about them immediately. Award-winners and thumb suckers alike, stories faded in the rearview mirror like so much clutter along life's road. With any luck, we'd keep the commercials from slamming together forever.

But never, ever, go more than 45 seconds.

www.ingramcontent.com/pod-product-compliance
Lightning Source LLC
Chambersburg PA
CBHW070503120726
47910CB00003B/1104